EDELWEISS

Book 3

Lloyd Hall

CUPERTINO, CA

Wardenclyffe Series
PO Box 2918
Cupertino, CA 95015
www.wardenclyffeseries.com

Cover Design © 2025 **Abigail Spence**
Interior Illustrations © 2025 **Minna Ollikainen**

Edelweiss/Lloyd Hall. -- 1st ed.
ISBN 978-1-7373919-6-8

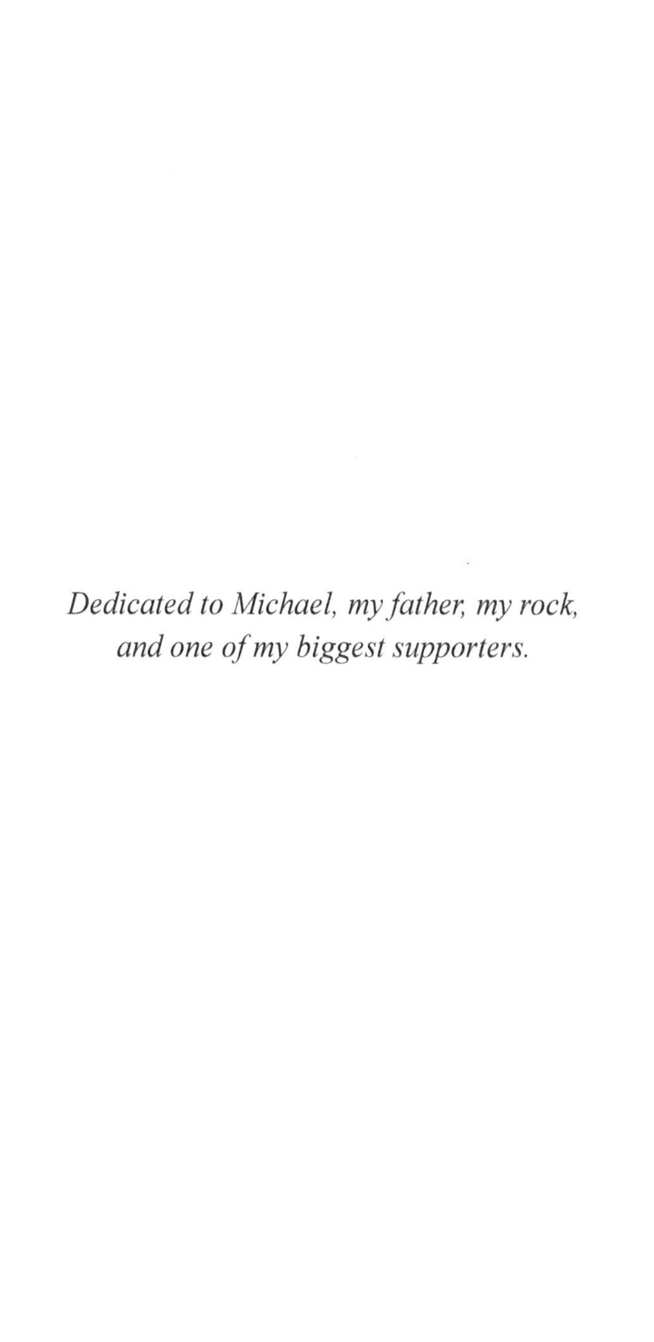

Dedicated to Michael, my father, my rock, and one of my biggest supporters.

CONTENTS

CHAPTER ONE

NEW HOME

"Here, take this." My dad places a wooden box into my hands.

"What is it?" I turn it over and examine the intricate carvings covering the surface. The lid is attached with bright gold hinges and secured with a buckle.

"It's a holo-recorder. Picked it up on the way to grab you." He leans over and opens the box for me. Nestled inside the velvet interior are small rows of clear discs, each with their own slot. On top of them sits a small metal machine about the size of my fist. I take the machine out and run my hands over the polished surface. Smooth.

"How's it work?" I turn it over.

"Press the button," he says, and I do. The machine hums, vibrating in my hands. I lift one end of it to my eyes and look through, before quickly realizing it's backwards and trying the other way. Through the lens I see the interior of the bus around me, with all the other passengers. There's a weird blue tint and it's a little fuzzy, like I'm looking through running water.

I turn around the room and start recording everything, but the dim lights make it pretty hard to make out any details. And thank god this thing can't pick up smells because I definitely don't want to remember all of these.

"Looks a little weird," I say as I press the button to stop the recording.

"Yeah, well, it's recording a holographic image! Trust me, when you play these back, they'll look just like the real thing," he assures me.

That's when I get an idea. "I'm gonna head up to the upper deck and get a better view," I say, jumping up from my seat.

"Ok, just be careful up there."

He smiles as I pull my coat down from the overhead compartment and slide my arms inside. I tie it closed and pull the fur-lined hood up over my head before carefully slipping the holo-recorder into my pocket. The stairs to the upper deck are steep and uncomfortable and, unhelpfully, the bus shakes violently as I climb. I make it to the landing and open the door to the deck. It slams loudly and I hear the noise echo back down the staircase.

I raise my arm and shield my eyes from the brightness outside. Feeling around for the door, I carefully step out onto the deck of the bus and close it behind me. It takes a few seconds for my eyes to adjust to the light. I walk past a bunch of other people standing around the deck in their big coats as I make my way over to one of the railings.

The icy landscape stretches out in every direction and the giant treads of the bus kick up a flurry of snow behind us. I pull out the holo-recorder and hold it up to my eyes, the blue tint making all the ice look like the ocean back home, with the illusion only disrupted by one giant black spire reaching up from the ice ahead of us.

I feel a hand on my shoulder and turn to see my dad standing next to me, now bundled in his big old coat. I think it's his only one, and at this point it's mostly held together with patches, the last few buttons hanging on by nothing more than their threads.

"What is that thing out there?" I ask, pointing at the spire.

"Not really sure. Probably been in the ice for hundreds of years," he says.

I turn the holo-recorder back to it as the bus passes closer. The spire looks like it's made from some dark metal, stretching up from the ice with sharp, jagged edges. The ice around it also looks dark, like whatever the spire is attached to stretches deep below the surface. But most surprisingly, as the sun hits it, there doesn't seem to be any glimmer off

the surface. It's like all the light just gets absorbed into its dark silhouette. It seems so sad just left in the ice like that.

"How can no one know what it is?" The spire gets smaller as we continue on and I turn the holo-recorder off once it's completely out of view.

"Well, it's probably from before the flooding. My guess is there's probably some archeology grad student back in University who's busy submitting a proposal to excavate it as we speak. But even so, there are very few people who actually understand all that old tech," he says.

I slip the holo-recorder back into my coat pocket. "Except you, right?" I joke.

"I certainly try." He chuckles. I love that deep laugh of his.

"ENTERING OLD HARBOR NOW." A loud announcement cuts through the old speakers on the deck of the bus. It's so full of static it's almost impossible to make out the words.

"Looks like we've got about another hour until we arrive. I'm gonna head back below deck and warm up, you wanna come?" he asks.

I shake my head. "Nah, I'm gonna keep watch up here." He smiles and walks over to the door as I turn back to the icy landscape. The cold bites at my face and I pull my hood tight. Despite how uncomfortable it is, I can't bring myself to leave the deck for fear of missing something exciting, like some new adventure waiting out in the ice for me.

I think about what my Dad said about the spire in the ice. Maybe I could do my own research trip out there someday. I'd probably have to study in University if I wanted to do something like that. But maybe I can be the next Florence Singh, discover my own underwater city or something cool like that. Dad read her book to me when I was a kid and I remember wanting to be just like her.

I turn away from the landscape and look around at the other passengers, trying to imagine why they're coming all the way out here. Most of them are dressed casually, except for one woman near the front of the bus who's wearing a deep red coat and large hat. I can't even remember the last time I saw anyone wearing such a bright shade of red. My dad says no one knows how to make that dye anymore so the coat must be pretty old, like an antique.

"ARRIVAL SOON." The speaker cuts me off mid-thought. Any ideas I may have had about the woman in the red coat are drowned out by the static of the speakers. There's a glowing spot in the distance ahead of us and I pull out the holo-recorder. I hold the railing and walk up to the front of the deck, trying to get a better view of what we're approaching.

We near the large hillside and the details of a massive city come into view. Hundreds of buildings are built into the side of the hill, stacked on top of each other, stretching far up the hillside. We quickly pass by a large white building that sits further outside the city on its own rocky outpost.

"Beautiful, isn't it?"

I turn quickly. It's the woman in the red coat, standing next to me, starting at the sprawling city in front of us.

"Uh, yeah." I don't really know what to say. She looks at me through the lens of the holo-recorder, which I promptly lower, meeting her gaze. Her eyes are friendly, a deep shade of brown, and her face is absolutely gorgeous. She doesn't seem fazed by the cold breeze.

"Shouldn't you be getting back to your seat?" She winks at me. I look around and notice all the other passengers on the deck have disappeared. I nod awkwardly and run back over to the door, quickly climbing down the stairs and back to my seat.

"You have fun up there?" Dad asks.

"I saw the city." I hold my hands against my face and try to warm myself up a little bit.

"What did you think?"

"It's so big. Much bigger than home." A beeping sounds from my pocket and I take out the holo-recorder. "What's it doing?"

"That disc's out of space. Here, let me show you." He opens the wooden box it came in and takes out another disc. "You can only record about an hour on each one." He opens the top of the holo-recorder and switches the clear discs inside, returning the old one to an empty slot in the box.

As he's putting the disc in, the bus rumbles loudly to a stop. Everyone gets up and begins to grab their belongings from the racks above their seats.

"Here, keep this with you." My dad hands me the box and I slip it into my empty pocket, the holo-recorder already tucked safely in the other. He passes down my suitcase before grabbing his own and slinging it onto his back. I forgot how much stuff I had in here. Maybe I should've packed a little lighter.

We make our way back up the staircase to the top deck along with the other passengers, everyone now bundled up warmly for the cold weather as they lug their baggage behind them. I walk outside and see that we've pulled up near a large ramp that has been extended out to meet the deck of the bus.

I step onto the wooden ramp, following closely behind the rest of the crowd as we walk down to the main dock. Down where the dock meets the land is a giant wooden archway with a sign that reads "Welcome to June", accompanied by a large crowd waiting underneath. I quickly scan through the crowd and see my mom waiting for us. I drop my suitcase and run up to give her a massive hug.

"Hey, Olive, glad you two made it up safely." She pulls me into a big embrace and I sink into her puffy coat.

"Missed you lots." I feel Dad join the hug behind me. We all stand there for a minute before I pull away. Dad places my suitcase next to me as another person steps forward to greet us. She's short, almost my height, and wearing an oversized wool coat. Her face is old and wrinkled and mostly hidden behind a large pair of dark glasses.

"Hello, Desmond, glad to have you back." She reaches out and shakes my dad's hand.

"Glad to be back," he says, before turning to introduce her to me. "Kai, this is my daughter Olivia."

Kai reaches out and shakes my hand too. "Nice to finally meet you, Olivia." Her hand feels warm. "I've heard so much about you from your parents."

"Kai works up here with me," Dad chimes in. "She's the one who helped us get settled into our new place."

"Nice to meet you too." I grab my suit-case from the ground next to me.

"Oh, you don't have to worry about that," Kai says, as a person appears next to us, startling me. His skin looks like it's completely made from metal, and he's dressed in a weird grey uniform. I look closer at his face and notice tiny screws.

"Are you an android?" I ask. I've heard of androids but I've never seen a working one in person before. All the ones near us stopped working long before I was born.

He nods. "That is correct." His voice is rough and robotic, full of static, like the speakers on the bus.

"I'm Olivia, what's your name?" I ask. Kai and my parents laugh.

"It doesn't have a name, sweetie," Kai explains. "It's just here to help with your bags." The android leans down, picks up my bag, then grabs my dad's.

"We're gonna bring these back to the house so you two can explore the city a little bit." Mom leans in and gives me a kiss on the cheek, then she kisses Dad. "See you back at the house a little later," she says, walking back along the dock. The android walks behind her with our bags hanging over his shoulders. In the crowd, I see a number of similar-looking androids helping people with luggage and they all have exactly the same face. It's a little strange.

"So, you two ready for the tour?" Kai asks.

"Absolutely!" To say I'm excited to explore this new city would be a complete understatement.

"Good! Let's head out then," she says.

I follow her and my dad along the dock towards the town. At the end of the wooden dock, we pass under the large wooden sign and step onto a cobblestone street. Massive stone steps stretch far up through the city above us and tall wooden pillars line either side. Detailed animals are carved into the pillars, each painted with brightly colored paint.

"How many people live here?" I ask as we walk by a series of wooden buildings.

"Easily a couple thousand," Kai answers.

"It's one of the biggest cities left," Dad says with a smile. I know he's happy to finally be living here. After all, he's been talking about moving up here for years.

We walk along the cobblestone street, past more of the wooden buildings, each one made from massive logs that are nearly twice my height. Unlike the buildings back home, all the wood here seems to have a reddish tint to it. The streets are bustling with people. We stop at a snowy courtyard, beyond which sits a large building built into the side of the hill.

"I thought you might like to see this place," Dad says, pointing at the building.

"Why, what is it?" I ask. There's no sign.

"It's your new school!" he says excitedly.

"My school?" I look at the building again. It's at least ten times the size of our old house and seems to be connected to a series of other small buildings.

"Yeah, the classes start next week, so you'll be able to get a little settled before you start," he says.

I guess I'll have to get used to the size of that place, but I'm excited to explore it more. We double back and stop at another set of large steps.

"Let's go up here," Kai says. We walk up the stone steps together, continuing past another street with more buildings, and finally stop at the street after that.

"This is a good spot for you to know," Dad says as we start walking down this cobblestone street.

"Why?" I look around at the buildings, but they look pretty much the same as all the others, except that each one has something carved into the wood above the doorway.

"This is where all the food shops are," he explains. We stop in front of a building that has a large fish carved above the door. Is this just a store for fish? My question is answered when we walk inside and see a large room filled entirely with various types of fish, which I can't even begin to identify, all sitting in large containers of ice. There's a woman at a table in the center of the room who's in the middle of carving up the biggest fish I've ever seen.

"It's a fish shop," I say.

Dad chuckles. "I thought we'd pick up some stuff for dinner along the way." He walks up to the woman carving the fish and starts talking to her.

Kai leans into me. "There are also a lot of other places in June that might be a little more up your alley," she says.

"Like what?" I ask.

She smiles. "Well, there's the city library."

My ears perk up when she says this. A library? "Where's that?" I ask eagerly, and she laughs.

"I'll take us by it on the way to your place."

My dad comes back over with a large cut of fish wrapped in paper and neatly tied with a piece of twine.

"Got us something fresh!" he says proudly. "Let's keep going."

I follow him out of the building and back onto the street. We pass by more crowds and the occasional android until we stop in front of another building. Dad quickly goes into this one and I rush in after him, with Kai trailing behind.

A wave of heat hits me the minute I step inside. Large red lights hang from the ceiling and every surface of the shop is covered with plants. There's a man wearing a green striped apron and carrying a small watering can who my dad promptly walks up to and starts discussing the plants in jars along the walls.

"So, what do you do?" I ask Kai.

"I'm the caretaker of the lighthouse," she says. We sit in some of the chairs while Dad shops around and chats with the owner.

"Yeah, I kind of knew that. But, like, what does that actually mean?" I watch as my dad pulls small jars off the shelf and looks closely at them.

"Well, the caretaker position is essentially a scientific residency, and my particular area of research was in geology, specifically studying the unique properties of some newly discovered minerals around June. But my tenure is up and it's time to pass the torch to someone else." She looks over at my dad.

"My dad?"

"Yes, each caretaker is responsible for picking the next. And out of all the applications I saw, his was by far the most interesting."

He walks back over with a small bag from the shopkeeper, who waves at us with a big smile. "What're you two talking about?" he asks as we get up from the chairs.

"We were talking about you becoming the caretaker," I say.

"Oh really?" he says as we leave the shop.

"Yeah, and Kai was telling me about what kind of work she did."

"Lots of rock talk," she explains. We keep walking down the street and stop at another set of stairs. "Hope you two are up for a climb."

I find my breath short in the cold air as we pass street level after street level until it feels like we've climbed a thousand steps. Finally, we stop. I turn back to look out over the city below us, then pull the holo-recorder out of my pocket. I start recording, making sure to capture as much of the view as I can through the lens. I turn it towards Kai and Dad, and they both wave awkwardly to the camera before I stop the recording.

"We're here," Dad says, stopping at a small building a little ways down the street. It's two stories and looks a little run down. Some of the shutters look like they're hanging on by a thread, and parts of the roof have seen better days. But still, something about it is kind of cute, and it's definitely way bigger than our last place.

"Welcome to our new home." He walks over to the door and steps inside. The front door is thick, with deep patterns etched into the wood and a carved wooden handle so thick my fingers can barely close around it.

I step over the threshold and I'm greeted by a warm, cozy room covered wall-to-wall in wood paneling and a large stone hearth on the opposite side, with a fire raging inside of it. Small lights buzz softly with electricity all around. My mom emerges from another room and comes over to greet us again.

"Hope you had a nice tour," she says. "And now that both of you are up here you can finally help me get settled into this new place." She gestures to the piles of crates we had sent up about a month ago, very few of which seem to have been unpacked. I walk over to some of them and look at the paper labels attached to the top. Most of them say things like 'Books' or 'Papers', some are labeled with stuff for the kitchen. I see one that says 'Olive' on it and pick it up. It's pretty heavy and the stuff inside clatters around loudly.

"This one's mine," I say.

"Oh good, let me show you your new room." Mom leads me out of the living area and down a narrow hallway lined with various doors. I follow her up the staircase at the end of the hall, each wooden step creaking loudly as I climb. Everything in this house feels old and has a musty smell to it. We reach the top of the stairs and emerge into another hallway.

Mom stops in front of one of the doors. "This one's yours."

"Really?" I set down the wooden crate.

"Yup."

The ornate brass knob is cold to the touch and clicks quietly as I turn it. The room is almost twice as big as the one back home. A thick layer of dust coats everything but I barely notice because my attention is quickly drawn to the large bay window.

"It's incredible." And in case the window wasn't cool enough already, the view takes my breath away. The room looks down over the buildings and streets of the city and the massive ice shelf stretching far into the distance beyond.

"We thought you'd enjoy the view," Mom says. "The place still needs a little cleaning up but we think it's gonna be really nice." She brings the crate of my stuff in and sets it down on a small desk in the corner. "How about you get settled then come down and join us for some food?"

"Sounds good," I say. My brain is only half present, and my mom smiles as she heads back downstairs, her footsteps getting fainter as she walks down the creaky staircase.

I'm still completely enthralled by the view. It's much better than the dirt yard my old room used to look over. I pull out the holo-recorder and point it out the window, even though I doubt this recording will be able to do it justice. After recording the view for a bit, I spin the device back towards the room and record everything, before turning it towards me.

"So… my dad just gave me this new holo-recorder. Not really sure what I should record on it… but I guess I'll just record whatever I want to…" I smile awkwardly at the lens. Feels weird to be talking to nothing like this. I switch it off and toss it onto the bed, then take off my coat and toss that down too. I walk over to the crate with my stuff in it, open the lid, and start taking things out.

My archery medal from camp, a stack of books I begged Dad to get me, a small jar of shells from the old beach back home. There are deep bookshelves on the walls next to the bay window where I place the books. And since I can't think of a better place for it right now, I place the jar of shells there too, using it to hold up the end of a row of books. There's a small door on the other side of the room, which I walk over to and pull open. My clothes are neatly hung up and organized inside the small closet. I can tell my mom must have unpacked these since the organization has her fingerprints all over it.

I close the closet and hang the small archery medal on the doorknob. I can hear voices coming faintly from downstairs and smell the rich scent of food wafting up the hallway towards my room. I can't quite place the smell but I feel my stomach growling so I make my way back downstairs.

"Hey, sweetie! What do ya think of your new digs?" Dad asks from across the living room. I walk over and find him standing in a small kitchen preparing food.

"It's pretty incredible," I say. He's got a cooked plate of the fish we picked up at the shop earlier.

"I knew you'd like it." He walks into the living room and places a few plates of food onto the low table where Kai is sitting. I walk over and sit down on the cushion next to her.

Kai leans into the fish and smells it. "Food smells incredible, Desmond."

"Yeah, Dad's an incredible cook," I add. He and my mom join us at the table and the four of us dig in.

"This tastes amazing," I say. "I don't even recognize most of the flavors." The food melts in my mouth.

"Yeah, they've got a bunch of different plants that grow up here," my dad explains. "Means a lot of the dishes have flavors like we don't have back home." He places another portion onto my already empty plate. I keep eating. I can't imagine I'll ever get sick of food this good. We spend the next couple of minutes eating in silence before a question occurs to me,

"When do you start work?"

He smiles and finishes chewing. "First thing tomorrow. But after we eat, Kai was going to show me to the research center." He pauses and takes a drink before smiling at me. "You want to come check it out with us?"

I feel butterflies in my stomach. "Yes please!"

"Well, go grab your coat from upstairs. We'll head out in a little bit." Before the words have fully left his mouth, I'm already running back up to my room. I grab the coat off the bed, revealing the holo-recorder underneath. Better bring that too. I pick it up and rush back downstairs.

"That was quick," Dad jokes as I pull my coat on. He leisurely puts his coat and shoes on and I can feel him dragging it out just because he knows how excited I am. He finally gets his stuff together and I pull him out the door by his coat.

"Come *on*." I tug at his arm.

Kai is waiting for us outside where the sun has already started to set. "You two ready to go?"

"Yes!" I say excitedly. She laughs and begins walking down the street as my dad and I follow. I look back and our house has already blended in with the others. Our last house was so distinct but all these look exactly the same; it's gonna take some getting used to.

As I'm looking around, Kai catches my attention and waves me over.

"You see that building ahead of us?" She points to a large building on the other side of the road, much bigger than most of the others and made from the biggest wooden beams I've ever seen. It almost looks like it extends up to the street level above this one.

"Yeah, what is it?" I ask.

She smiles. "That's the library I was telling you about."

I peek in through the windows and see stacks of books stretching far back, more than I've ever seen in one place before. I don't even think University has this many. Once we're all settled, I'm totally coming back to check it out.

We descend the stone stairs and I count the levels as we pass each one, until finally we stop a few levels above the ice shelf. To my left, the street stretches out of the town, winding along the edge of the mountains, and ending at a massive white building. Kai leads us down the street and as we reach the edge

of town, the cobblestones fade into a narrower dirt path with a dusting of snow over it.

"Not too much further now," Kai says as
we approach the tall, white building. Its
bright white stone, which glistens brightly in
the setting sun, really sets it apart from all the
other buildings in town. The shadow it casts
looms over us as we walk up the front steps.

"Here we are!" My dad gestures up at it.
"Welcome to the Wardenclyffe lighthouse."
He walks up the steps to the metal door and
pulls it open with another grand gesture. Set
into the stone above the door is a large metal
sign which reads WARDENCLYFFE
LIGHTHOUSE.

"Why's it called a lighthouse?" I ask, following him inside.

"Well, it was built hundreds of years
ago," Kai explains. "The story is that it was
designed to guide ships safely back home."
She follows me inside and shuts the door behind us. "But there haven't been ships up this
way in a really long time."

I guess that's probably true; the busses
are likely the only thing that can actually
make it over the ice shelf anymore.

The inside of the lighthouse is even
weirder than the outside. The room we've just
stepped into is shaped like a giant octagon,
with tables set up everywhere. There's a fire-

place on one side and a large metal staircase in the middle leading up through the ceiling.

"Hey, Olive, I've got some paperwork to fill out. Feel free to take a look around," Dad says. I'm so distracted by all the stuff in the room I barely even notice him take a seat at one of the tables with Kai. They've got a stack of papers in front of them that looks like it's going to keep them occupied for a little while.

"I'm gonna look upstairs." I glance over at the spiral staircase.

"That's fine, I just ask that you don't touch anything up in the lab," Kai says.

I nod and climb up the spiral staircase, stepping out onto the next floor, which is filled with a bunch of random bookshelves and tables. I walk around the room and look over the books on the shelves. They've all got really weird titles like *The Grid: a modern-day power system* and *A Brief History of the Salmon* to name a few. I continue past the bookcases and stop at the wall of the room.

It's coated with hundreds of wires, so dense you can't even see the stone wall behind them. There's thin wood paneling laying all around the floor, which looks like it used to cover up the wires but has been sloppily ripped away, leaving them exposed. I look closer and notice they seem to stretch all the way from the floor below into the ceiling above. I walk back to the staircase and climb up to the next floor. It's pretty much the same as the one before, more wires along the walls and everything. I pull the holo-recorder out of my pocket and turn it on.

"Welcome to the Wardenclyffe lighthouse," I say as I spin the holo-recorder around the room. "There's a lot of old stuff around here." I pan across all the bookshelves in the room before making my way over to the staircase and climbing up another level. This floor has a small kitchen on one of the walls and looks more like a bedroom.

And sure enough, there's a bed in the corner, stacked with piles of quilted blankets and big fluffy pillows. At the foot of the bed there's a large wooden chest which, like many of the surfaces of the lighthouse, is stacked with books. There's also a big worn chair that, in my opinion, looks like it might actually be a cozier place to sleep than the bed. And from above the bed, bright light shines into the room through one of the windows.

"Would you look at that," I say into the recording. Outside the window, the surface of the ice shelf is painted in hues of orange by the sunset, like an oil painting. I click the recording off. I bet that looks incredible from the top of the building.

I run back over to the stairs and keep climbing. The next floor looks like a laboratory, very similar to Dad's in University. I stop and quickly look around. Kai said not to touch anything, but there's no harm in looking, right? The tables are stacked with clear containers, each one filled with various types of rocks. The ones that really catch my eye have large orange crystals inside, which shimmer brilliantly as the light catches them. The rest of the room is covered in loads of scientific equipment like microscopes sitting on all the tables.

I look around for another minute before making my way back to the stairs and climbing up the last couple of floors, not stopping to explore any of the others on my way. There's time for that later. I finally reach the last floor of the lighthouse. I don't know what I expected but it definitely wasn't this.

I'm standing at the edge of a large spherical room as the last glimpses of sunset filter through the hundreds of glass panels that make up the walls, completely bathing the room in a blinding orange light. From up here I can see far off into the distance over the ice shelf in one direction and, turning back, I can see the buildings of June behind me.

Large marble figures stand around the edges of the room facing inwards, each one a completely different person from the last. I pull out the holo-recorder and carefully move around the room, capturing their faces in the recording and wondering who they might be. Maybe they're the ones that built this place.

In the middle of the room there's a large blocky seat carved from the same marble as the statues. I walk over and take a seat. The stone is cold but the view is incredible, despite being slightly blocked by one of the statues directly in front of me. Embedded in the arms of the seat are long metal panels with a bunch of buttons. Pressing them does nothing so I kick my feet up over the arms of the seat and watch the sun set through the lens of the holo-recorder.

There's a soft beep from the recorder and the lens goes dark. There's a small red light flashing on its side. Guess it must be out of space. I switch it off and tuck it back into my pocket. I look back around the room again, just thinking how cool of a hideout this place would make. Maybe I could add a few plants. I'm sure Dad wouldn't mind if I start to make myself at home here.

LIBRARY

Something smells incredible. I roll over in my bed and slowly open my eyes. Light pours into my bedroom through the large window and I sniff the air. What is that incredible smell? I slowly sit up and feel around the floor for my slippers, sliding them awkwardly onto my feet when I eventually find them. I wonder how early it is.

I pull open the door to my room and step out into the hallway. It's super cold so I quickly make my way downstairs into the living room where luckily there's a fire going in the hearth. My mom and dad are sitting at the table in the middle of the room, bundled up in a big blanket.

"Hey, you're up early," Mom says. "You don't have to be at school for another couple of hours."

I look up at one of the old clocks on the wall. Oh yeah, it's way earlier than I needed to be up. "You guys are up," I say, sitting on one of the cushions around the table.

"Yeah, well, today's my official first day of work too," Dad says.

I grab a soft roll from a plate in the middle of the table and bite into it. "There are incredible," I say, crumbs falling out of my mouth.

"Use a plate." My dad slides a plate into my lap. He finishes the last of his food before standing up and taking his plate into the kitchen. I watch as he cleans it and neatly puts it away in the cupboards.

"Do you already know where all the dishes go?" I ask.

"Maybe." He smiles at me and walks over to the door. "Come give me a hug before I head out."

I run over and give him a huge hug. "Have a good day at work," I say.

He pats my head. "And you have fun at school. I wanna hear all about it later tonight, ok?" I nod in approval. He grabs his coat and is quickly out the door.

"So, what do you want to do before school?" Mom walks over to the kitchen, grabs Dad's plate from the cupboard where he left it and puts it into another one with all the other plates. She gives me a wink.

"I kind of want to explore a little bit," I say, thinking back to the library Kai showed me the other day.

"Grab some food before you head out, ok?" She gestures to the food on the table. I sit back down and she comes in with a tray of warm pastries from the kitchen. They've got large red chunks in the bread that I don't recognize.

"What's in this?" I smell it carefully. It's definitely what I was smelling from upstairs.

"I picked up some local berries from one of the market shops."

I bite into the pastry and it melts in my mouth. It's not a taste I'm familiar with but it's one of the most delicious things I've ever eaten. The berries alone are far sweeter than anything back home and balance out the dryness of the pastry perfectly.

"It's so good," I say once I've finished devouring every crumb. "All the food up here tastes incredible." I think back over the last couple of meals we've had up here, each better than the last.

"Yeah, this city is on a pretty major trade route so there's a lot of stuff we couldn't get before." She hands me another one of the pastries and I grab it quickly.

"Trade route?" I ask.

"Yeah, while I was waiting for you two to join me up here, I did some exploring of my own. You'd be surprised at some of the beautiful things you can find in the shops down in the market streets."

She stands up and brings her dishes over to the kitchen. I clear my plate and follow her over. We wash them together and she shows me where they go in the cabinets.

"Thanks for breakfast," I say.

"I'm gonna pack you some food for lunch while you get ready," she says.

I run back upstairs to get changed. The outfit I picked out yesterday is still hanging on the door of my closet. The pants are my favorite pair with a bright plaid pattern. I think it's gonna be a good school outfit, even if I'm still not really sure what people wear up here. I change into it and look at myself in the mirror.

Perfect. The gold buttons on my shirt catch the light as I spin back and forth. I tuck my hair behind my ears before deciding against that hairstyle and letting it fall down naturally again. I grab my coat and scarf from the closet and pull them on. I feel the lump of the holo-recorder box in my pocket. Good, I'll be needing that.

I run back downstairs and meet my mom in the kitchen. She's cutting up a bunch of food and placing it into a small wooden box for me. It looks like some kind of meat over rice. It's going to take all my restraint not to eat that food right away.

"Hey there, I'll be done in just a sec." She looks over at me. "Oh, you look cute," she says with a smile.

"Yeah?"

"Of course. You know I love that outfit." She smiles. Oh yeah, these pants used to be hers. I think that's probably why I like them so much.

"I thought it would be a good first impression," I say. She nods and hands me a small bag of the food she prepared.

"I absolutely agree. You remember where the school is?" she asks, and I nod.

"Yup, down on the lowest level." I grab my backpack from near the door and tuck the food inside.

"Good, don't be late getting there, ok?"

"I won't!" I look up at the clock. An hour and a half. That should be more than enough time to do some exploring. I run over and give my mom a big hug.

"Have a great day, honey."

"I will!" I rush out the door onto the bright street in front of our house.

Where to begin? It's so hard to decide, but I think the library has to be my first pick today. I head down the street, away from my house. I think I have a pretty good memory of where the library is. These buildings look exactly the same, but I remember it being bigger than the other ones and it wasn't too far, was it?

I stop. There it is. It's the biggest building on the street by far, looming over everything else. Large wooden pillars hold up the domed roof, each pillar so big it could've easily been a full tree. A large tower sits atop the entranceway with an ornately carved clock set into the face. I take in the details of the thick wooden doors as I approach, each one twice my height and carved with scenes of people. I wonder if there's any meaning behind all the details.

I pull open one of the doors and step inside the library. I'm greeted by a large entryway with massive ceilings stretching up above me. Light filters into the room through the narrow windows behind me, illuminating just how old and dusty everything is. I stifle a sneeze. Despite being dusty, I catch the familiar smell of old books and, for just a moment, I'm back in University again.

"You need help with anything?" A tall woman walks up to me. I can't quite tell how old she is; definitely older than me, but not as old as my mom. I think it's partly her outfit that's throwing me. She wears a long skirt with a woven shawl wrapped around her shoulders, all in dull, muted tones. Her hair is pulled back into a messy bun and in her arms

is a small stack of books, which she sets down on a nearby table.

"I was just looking around," I say, totally distracted by the room around me.

"You ever been here before?" She looks at me closely.

"Nope, just moved here," I say, shaking my head.

"Want a tour?" She gestures to the rest of the building.

"I'd love that!"

She leads me into a large atrium. "This is the main room of the library."

The floor is intricately tiled in a pattern that looks like a compass, and all around the room are comfy looking chairs that look worn and cozy from years of people sitting in them. A couple of people already seem to have settled into them for the day. I look up at the domed ceiling where large murals have been painted all around and light shines through a large circular window at the top.

"It's beautiful," I say, admiring the room.

"Yeah, and past here are the stacks." We walk to the other side of the atrium where there are rows and rows of bookshelves stretching further back than I can see.

"How far back does it go?" I walk along the aisle, looking down each one.

"Pretty far." She laughs. "The library's one of the oldest buildings here so it was actually built into the cliffside itself."

I look over at the walls and notice that they're completely made from stone. "Are a lot of buildings here like this?"

"Only the really old ones. There're rumors some of them stretch miles back into the mountain." For a second, she looks dead serious, then she laughs. "But those are mostly just old folk tales."

"Is it ok if I look around?" I ask.

"Of course! I'll leave you to it." She smiles and walks back towards the atrium. I step into one of the rows of bookshelves and walk down it. There are dim lights hanging from the stone ceilings. Every couple of seconds they flicker. Must be pretty old. These rows are also super narrow, like they tried to cram as many books into this space as possible.

There are a couple of other people browsing the stacks of books along with me.

"Excuse me," I say, awkwardly squeezing past one of them. The bookshelves seem to go on endlessly. There are small gold plaques on the shelves with the genres of books, many of which have begun to rust. Luckily most of them still seem to be readable. The one directly in front of me reads BIOGRAPHIES.

I pull one of the old books off of the shelf and look at the cover. *Piper Sato – Titan of Exploration*. I open the book and see a portrait of a woman in a white uniform. I flip through a couple pages. There're beautiful illustrations depicting everything from weird-looking plants to giant golden buildings. There's also a bunch of writing I don't recognize, and I wonder what language it's in.

I return that book to the shelf and pull out another one. *William Shakespeare – The Man Behind the Plays*. Oh, this guy I actually know. I remember reading some of his plays back in school. I slip the book back onto the shelf and keep walking down the aisle.

The bookshelves open up into another atrium, this one much smaller, and unlike the other one, there's no light coming in from above. Instead, there's just one dimly lit chandelier hanging from the ceiling and three old chairs in the corner of the room. This atrium has a number of paintings hanging inside and above them all is a large sign that says WARDENCLYFFE. It looks identical to the sign on the front of the lighthouse. A series of smaller tunnels lead off of this atrium with rows of books on either side.

The painting directly below the sign looks ancient. There's a crowd of people standing in front of the lighthouse, but instead of the ice shelf beyond it, there's a deep blue ocean. Is that what it used to look like here? I notice the librarian from before putting books back into the shelves nearby.

I walk over to her. "Can I ask you a question?"

"Of course you can. That's what I'm here for." She continues to place books back onto the shelf with a smile.

"When is that painting from?" I point over at the painting of the lighthouse.

"Oh, that? I don't know the exact date on that one, but I do know it's from before the flooding happened." She finishes putting the last book back into the shelves.

"How long has the lighthouse been here?"

"I'm not really sure on that either, sorry." She notices my disappointment. "But if you really want to know, I can look into it a bit."

"Really?"

She smiles. "Yeah, come back in a couple of days and I can let you know what I've found."

"Thanks so much! I totally will!" I say. She starts to walk back down the stacks. "I'm Olivia by the way," I call out to her.

She turns back to me. "That's a nice name. I'm Astrid." She gives another smile before walking back towards the atrium.

I look around at some of the other paintings in the room. All of them look just about as old as the one with the lighthouse. There's one that looks like a desert with dozens of tall, metal buildings. Another of a large city with a giant white statue of a person in the center. I look at the small plaques beneath each of these paintings. The first says THE SHIPYARD, the other one says MERCURY.

After looking at all the paintings, I pick one of the other paths off the atrium and keep walking down it. The lights in here are even dimmer than the rest of the library. The books look older and more worn too, all coated with an even thicker layer of dust. There's barely anyone else this far back in the aisles.

A small section of the bookshelves catches my eye. The dust in front of a few books has been cleared away, cleaned off by the books being pulled out. And sure enough, the books are completely free of dust too. Unlike some of the other shelves, this one has no plaques to label what all the books are about. The floor of this hallway also seems to be made from metal instead of stone like the rest of the library. My shoes echo as I step against it.

I pull one of the books off the shelf. *User Manual TR027*. I open the book and inside is an illustration of one of the androids I've seen around June. I skim through the table of contents. 'Introduction', 'Anatomy', 'Power & Charging', 'Voice Controls', 'Repairs'. I put that one back on the shelf and pull out another. *User Manual TR076 – Unreleased.* The cover of this one looks a lot more beat up so I'm very careful as I open it.

A number of the pages have been torn out, but luckily the table of contents is still there so I skim over the chapter names. 'Introduction', 'Power & Charging', 'AI Integration', 'Voice Controls', 'Discontinuation'. Nothing really jumps out. I put the book back onto the shelf. It seems like this is just a selection of user manuals for ancient tech.

I eventually reach the end of this hallway and come up against a large wall, the same material as the floors. I run my hands over the cold surface, looking for any interesting details but finding nothing more than a smooth surface everywhere. I turn around and start walking back, following the bookshelves towards the atrium, squeezing past more people as I leave. I wave to Astrid as I pass her, then I open the large wooden doors and step back outside onto the cold streets of June.

I look up at the large clock on the front of the library. Looks like I've still got an hour left until I have to be at school, plenty of time to do a little more exploring. I walk down the steps towards some of the food shops.

The streets are bustling with people, probably hundreds, all ducking into the shops then emerging again with bags of everything from food and flowers to clothing and tools, most also with androids in tow, carrying the bags for them.

My eye catches a glimpse of something bright red. I push through the crowd, trying to get a better look, until I finally see her. Wearing the same brilliant red coat is the woman I met on the deck of the bus. She weaves quickly and effortlessly through the crowd and, without really thinking about it, I find myself following her.

She turns down a new street towards a part of the city I haven't seen yet. I'm careful to keep a distance so she doesn't see me, but luckily her red coat makes her pretty easy to keep an eye on. The crowds are also much smaller here, although I do notice more androids wandering around, seemingly on autopilot. They don't seem to be helping anyone at the moment.

The paint on the buildings in this area is faded and many look completely abandoned. I keep following the woman until we're on a small street with almost no one else around, save for a handful of androids. I notice a couple of them have different faces than the others I had seen throughout town. Maybe they're other models?

I watch one of the androids walk into a building and the woman follows him inside. I run up to the building and peer through one of the windows. It's dusty and hard to see through but I can still make out the red from the woman's coat. She goes deeper into the building and I move to one of the other windows, trying to get a better view. A couple of people passing by give me odd looks but quickly move on.

It's still pretty hard to see through, but I notice a small alleyway next to the building. Jackpot. There's a little window about halfway up the wall that looks like it has a broken spot in it. I grab a small wooden crate laying nearby and prop it up near the window, then climb on top and pull myself up.

I can finally see clearly inside the building though the hole. The room, much like the building itself, looks completely abandoned. There are holes in the wood flooring, and piles of junk stacked up everywhere. The woman is kneeling over something on the other side of the room, but I can't quite make out what. I pull the holo-recorder out of my pocket and quietly turn it on.

I lift the recorder up to the window and hold it near the opening, trying to make sure it's getting a good view of her while also trying to stay as quiet as I possibly can. I peer through the crack in the window next to the holo-recorder.

There's a sudden beeping from the holo-recorder and she stands up quickly, looking around. I duck down but manage to catch a glimpse of something bright orange glowing in her hand. I listen to her inside the room and hear the footsteps moving away, then the front door opening again. From my spot in the alley, I see a flash of red as she passes by on the street. I stay hidden until I'm sure she's gone.

I turn the holo-recorder off and remove the disc. What an awful time for a reminder that the disc is full. I feel around in my pocket for another disc, which I swap back into the recorder. Then I climb down off the crate and walk around to the front of the building.

The door's unlocked so I carefully open it and step inside. Turns out there's even more junk in this room than I was able to see before. It looks like a bunch of old machinery. On the opposite wall there's a bunch of large displays with panels of buttons in front of them. I walk over to where the woman had been standing and see an android laying on the ground.

"Are you ok?" I kneel down beside him. There's a square panel on his chest that's completely open. It looks like something might have been inside but now there's just a bunch of random wires jutting out. I look at his face, the same face I've seen on all the other androids. His eyes are open but he's completely unresponsive. What did she do to him?

I close his eyes before standing up and looking around all the other piles of junk. I wonder what this building used to be. It feels like it must have been important at one point. I walk over to the wall of monitors and buttons and try pressing some but they don't seem to do anything.

As I'm busy pressing buttons, I think back to the books I saw in the library. What was that user manual one? It was for this android, right? I quickly leave through the front door and run back through all the crowds, up to the street where the library is. I pull open the door and step inside. Astrid notices me as I come in.

"Oh, back so soon?"

"Yeah, I just remembered a book I saw. Is it ok to borrow it?" I ask.

"Sure thing. Just bring it up here and I'll sign it out for you," she says.

I run back into the shelves until I reach the smaller atrium again. I look at all the paths branching off of it. Which one was it down again? I pick one at random and give it a try. No luck here.

I try another path. Bingo. I find the section where the books have been moved recently and pull out the one that says *User Manual TR027*. I tuck it under my arm and quickly squeeze my way past people in the stacks. I arrive back in the main atrium and run over to Astrid, who's now sitting at a small desk.

I place the book down in front of her.

"So, what've you got here?" She pulls out a small pair of glasses and puts them on. "An android user manual? Odd choice," she says, eyeing it closely. She pulls out a pen and writes the book's name in a large ledger sitting on the table.

"It caught my eye earlier," I say.

She smiles and hands the book back over to me. "Well, I hope you enjoy it."

I nod and tuck the book under my arm again. I leave through the front door and the second I get outside, I pull the book out and start leafing through it. I start with the introduction page.

Welcome to your new android. This is the user manual for the TR027 model, the 27th edition of the Transistor-brand androids. These series have all been carefully modeled after the old Hollywood actor Romero Hart, born July 8th 2192, star of such movies as Europa Strikes! *and* Love on the Event Horizon. *For any questions regarding other available—*

I flip ahead a few pages and stop when I see the section labeled 'Anatomy'. There's a large diagram of the android's body. I scan over and look at the chest. Sure enough, the drawing has the same chest panel as the one I had seen back in that building. I read the label 'Power Cell'. Huh, so that's the android's battery? Is that the glowing orange thing that the woman was holding?

As I'm reading, there's suddenly a loud chiming from above me. I quickly shut the book and look up. The clock tower on the library is ringing out through the town. I bet you can probably hear it from everywhere. That's when I notice the time.

9AM. Oh no. That's when school starts. I got completely distracted looking through this book and following that woman. I'm going to be so late for my first day. I start running down the street as fast as I can, turning and sprinting down the stone steps. I can see people's heads turning as I run but I eventually make it to the lowest street level.

It looks like another bus just pulled into the port. I see a bunch of people walking along the docks towards this level. I'm so distracted I run directly into someone on the street. I fall over my feet and my face plants directly into the cobblestones. I pull myself up, holding my nose – luckily it doesn't seem to be bleeding but it certainly hurts a lot.

"Hey, sorry about that." I look up at the person I ran into. It's one of the androids.

"For what are you sorry?" he asks.

"For running into you!" I say. I slowly get back onto my feet. "Must've hurt a bit!"

"I do not feel pain. There is no need for concern," he says. Then, with no further words, he turns and walks towards the docks. All the androids I've met so far feel really odd, and while I don't think I'm quite used to having them around yet, I definitely want to learn more about them.

The ice sheet stretches out next to me as I rush along the street. I recognize most of these buildings from when we first arrived in the city. And luckily the layout makes it pretty easy not to get lost, which is helpful since I do have a tendency to get lost when I go exploring.

I stop when I catch something out of the corner of my eye. Down on the ice shelf there's a bunch of people working on something. I walk over to the edge of the street to get a better look. From what I can tell they seem to be clearing off the snow from a large section of the ice. I see a couple of others watching the people work. I walk up to them and notice Kai among the crowd.

"Hey, Kai, do you know what's going on down there?" I ask.

"Oh, hey, Olivia. Good to see you again. Yeah, they're clearing it off for ice skating," Kai explains.

"I've never heard of ice skating before." I keep watching the people clear the ice.

"You should try it! Bring some friends, it's a lot of fun. Plus, this is the first time they've set it up in like twenty years. Feels like a special occasion," she says with excitement.

"I totally will! That sounds super cool!"

"Hey, shouldn't you be in school?" Kai says with a smile.

"Oh crap." I got completely distracted again. I wave to Kai and run back along the path to the school again. I'm absolutely going to come back and check out that ice skating thing though. It sounds like a lot of fun.

I see the school ahead of me, and I run into the courtyard, up to the main building. I glance up at the large clock on the front; ten minutes late. Not the way I wanted to start my first day in a new school.

CHAPTER THREE

FIRST DAY

The old doors to the school creak loudly as I push them open. Inside there are a bunch of kids all my age walking around. I can't ever remember seeing this many people my age all at once, practically everyone in University is older.

I pull out the small map of the school that was given to me yesterday. It's a little wrinkled from being in my pocket all morning but I press it flat and try to find where I need to go. The school has six main buildings, which seem to be connected by a labyrinth of tunnels and passages. Directly in front of me are stairs leading down into one of the tunnels. I check the map again and it looks like these should take me to the building I need to be in for class.

I walk down the stairs and find myself in a long underground tunnel, almost exactly like the one in the library, just without all the bookshelves. There's a static noise, then I hear someone's voice echoing loudly though the tunnel.

"Class is beginning in three minutes," the voice says.

I stop one of the other kids in the hallway. "Hey, which way to the art building?" I ask.

"Down the hall, then left, then right, then another right," they say, before rushing off past me. I run down the hallway as quickly as I can. When I come to a split, I turn down the left path, run along it, then come to another split where I turn right.

Every single one of these hallways looks the same, just dirt floors and dim lights. I don't know how I'm supposed to tell any of them apart. Couldn't they at least put up signs? There also doesn't seem to be any other students around that I can ask for more directions, probably since they're all in class by now.

I reach another fork in the tunnel and think back to what the other kid told me. Was it left or right here? I can't remember. Well, it's a fifty-fifty chance, right? I turn down the left hallway and keep running. It opens up into a large room covered from floor to ceiling in blue and white tiles. There's a hole in the center of the room, also covered in the same tiles, and little metal ladders on each side. This is weird. Almost instinctively, I pull out the holo-recorder and start recording as I walk around the exterior. It looks like it hasn't been used in a while.

On the opposite side of the room, there's another set of stairs leading up. I climb them, thinking the art building may be on the other side of this weird room, however at the top of the stairs I find myself in a large open space that's very clearly not the art building. I turn around and get a full view of everything with the holo-recorder.

A layer of thick grass grows across the floor. I think it's actually the first grass I've seen since moving up to June. Two large nets sit on either side of the room, both rusting and overgrown with plants. The grass comes almost up to my knees as I push through to a tunnel on the other side. There's a small rope hanging across the entrance to the tunnel, which I quickly slip under.

Unlike the others, the lights in this tunnel are barely working. I can only see a few feet ahead of me, but I make sure to keep the holo-recorder pointed forwards. I feel like my first day of school should be well-documented. This tunnel has a series of doors along it. I pull the handle of one of them but it doesn't budge.

I try the next one; still no luck. Luckily the third one opens easily, although there's no light inside. I feel around the wall for some kind of light switch until I eventually find one and I turn it on. A bright light lights up the tiny room. Along the wall is a series of monitors and boards with buttons on them. They look identical to the ones I saw in that abandoned building earlier today, but these ones look like they might still work.

I walk over and try pressing some of the buttons. No response on these ones either. I turn the light off and walk back out. I keep walking down the hallway when suddenly my foot hits something that makes a loud CLANG noise. I look down. The floor in this area is much different. Unlike the dirt and rock of the previous tunnels, this is completely metal from floor to ceiling.

After a couple more steps, the hallway suddenly lights up. I shield my eyes. Once they adjust to the brightness, I can clearly make out the details of the hallway, polished metal everywhere and a large metal bulkhead a few feet away, completely blocking off the rest of my path. I examine it closely, making sure to capture all of this on the holo-recorder. It feels like the hallway should keep going but there doesn't seem to be any way past this wall. There's a small piece of metal near one side that almost looks like a door handle, so I reach for it.

"You there!" calls a voice from behind that almost makes me jump out of my skin. I turn around and see a man standing behind me with a flashlight. "What're you doing out here?"

"I'm looking for the art building," I tell him. He's wearing a fancy suit and tie. His head is completely bald and he's very tall.

"These tunnels are off limits. Come with me." He turns and starts walking back down the tunnel.

"I didn't know," I say, following him. We duck back under the rope and enter the grass-covered room again.

"What did you think this rope meant?" he asks.

"I didn't really think about it." I follow him back through the grass, each of our footsteps leaving deep impressions where we walk.

"Well, you should have."

He's not a very friendly guy, is he? We pass back through the tiled room and into the hallway I had come from, except this time, we go down the other path. Darn, must have been right instead of left. We arrive at another staircase and climb it up into a different building, probably the art one if I had to guess. The man leads me past a dozen wooden doors before stopping in front of one of them and opening it for me.

"In you go." I step into the room and he shuts the door behind me.

Light from outside filters in through the large windows, making the room feel cozy and warm. A person stands on a small platform in the middle of the room, and around them sit a bunch of other kids with easels, all drawing the figure with large chunks of black charcoal.

"Who're you?" A big burly man walks up to me. He's got a large beard, thick glasses, and an apron that's covered in colorful paint stains.

"I'm Olivia. I'm here for the class," I explain. "Sorry I'm late." I look around at everyone else, but they pay me little mind.

"No worries, Olivia. I'm Tim, the teacher for this class." He pulls a small block of charcoal out of one of the large pockets on his apron. "Grab a seat," he says, handing it to me. The charcoal feels weird against my fingers and the more I hold it, the more of a mess it seems to make. I sit down at one of the empty chairs in front of an easel and pull my coat off. With how warm this room feels, I definitely don't need it. The other kids stay focused on the person on the platform, who I notice hasn't moved a muscle since I walked in.

"Let's use this as a chance to change poses," Tim says. Everyone flips over their drawings to a new page and I stare at the blank one in front of me. Am I just supposed to start

drawing? The person on the platform finally unfreezes and turns to face me. It's a girl about my age, absolutely stunning, with dark brown hair flowing past her shoulders.

But the most striking part about her is the absolutely ridiculous costume she's wearing. She's being drowned by an oversized patchwork coat, a cacophony of mis-matched fabrics and bright colors. Around her neck is a frilly collar and atop her head sits a large picture hat. Not a single piece of the ensemble looks like it goes together but nonetheless, she strikes a new pose and the class begins sketching.

"Ok, we'll take five minutes on this pose," Tim says. He walks around and stares at everyone's pieces as they draw.

I grab the charcoal and lift it up to the paper. I try to sketch the girl in the costume, starting with her big hat, but every line I draw feels wobbly and uneven. I manage to get the rough shape onto the page, then I pause and look up at her again for reference. Our eyes meet. I quickly look away, my face turning a bright shade of red. I glance up again, but this time she's looking off into the distance. My rugged charcoal lines really don't do her features justice. I wish I could capture her likeness better. A thought occurs to me and I pull out the holo-recorder from my coat pocket.

I flip the switch on and point it up at her. The sunlight from the windows silhouettes her perfectly in the light, giving her an ethereal glow, one that I know my piece of charcoal could never do justice. Our eyes meet again. I give an awkward smile before fumbling and awkwardly dropping the holorecorder. It clatters onto the ground loudly, drawing the attention of the class.

"Sorry about that," I say, kicking it under my coat before anyone notices it. Tim walks over and looks at my sloppy drawing.

"You seem a little distracted," he says. I pick up the charcoal again and continue drawing, moving on to the frilly collar, then to the coat, trying my best to just get the shapes right. I glance at the easel next to me. Their drawing is clearly way more polished than mine, even capturing the textures of all the different fabrics of the patchwork.

Just as I feel like I'm getting into the swing of sketching, Tim raises his hand. "That's time," he says, and everyone puts their charcoals down. The girl up on the pedestal unfreezes from her pose again. "And thanks to Ava for being our volunteer today."

She steps down off the platform and walks over to one of the tables in the room. Piece by piece, she pulls off her ensemble, leaving them in a large pile and revealing a perfectly cute outfit underneath it all.

Tim walks around the room and hands us each a thick book with a dark red cover and fancy gold lettering, the words *22nd Century Art History Retrospective* embossed into the leather. Ava takes a seat in the last open chair next to me.

"I'm Olivia." I lean closer to her.

She looks up at me and gives me a long stare before responding. "Ava," she says as Tim hands her one of the books. She looks away from me and stares intently at the book. I look back at mine too as Tim takes his place at the front of the class.

"Ok, everyone, welcome to Art History. We'll be learning about some of the major art movements of the past couple hundred years, beginning with the twenty-second century." He opens the book. "And as I said before, we'll be starting each class with warm up-drawings. I think to truly understand the art, it's important to experience the materials used."

I look at the charcoal on my easel. I guess that's why we were doing the warm-up sketches.

"So, before I start lecturing, can anyone tell me about the Return-To-Nature art movement, which began in the early twenty-second century?" There's a moment of silence in the class before Ava raises her hand. "Yes, Ava?"

"It was an artistic movement about shunning the digital medium and using naturally occurring materials to create paintings and sculpture," she says quietly.

"That's absolutely correct! Anyone know what some of those materials were?" He looks around the room and no one answers. "I'll give you all a hint, it's one I know you all have used before." He gives a slight smile to the room.

"OH!" I say.

He turns towards me. "You know what it is, Olivia?"

"Is it charcoal?" I pick up a stick of the black charcoal from the easel.

"That's correct! Charcoal was absolutely one of the materials they used, along with natural paints, clay, wood, sand, rock, wool, and a number of others." He holds up the book. "So, if you all want to follow along, you can open up to the first chapter of this book."

I open my copy to the first chapter, called 'Return-To-Nature (2120-2134)'. There's a photograph of a large painting that I've never seen before. I read the caption below.

One of the most prominent examples of the Return-To-Nature movement, this painting was created by the artist Georgia Englewood in 2122. It was one of the first of her Return-

To-Nature era which eventually led to the revival in physical artworks, leading to other later movements such as the Romanesque Refresh, TechArt, and even the Retroist movement.

I don't think I've ever heard of any of this stuff before. I learned some history in University, but it was mostly stuff my dad was already studying, never artsy stuff like this. I'm actually kind of excited for this class.

Tim begins his lecture while most of the other kids follow along in the book. Ava sits next to me, reading the book intensely. After about an hour of talking about the various artistic movements, Tim closes his book.

"Well, I think that's enough for today," he says. "It's about time for the next classes anyways."

Everyone in the room begins to pack up their stuff. I grab my coat from the floor and pick up the holo-recorder that I had kicked under it earlier, then grab my bag and look around for Ava but she's already gone. I pull my class schedule out of my bag and glance over it. Science next.

"Anyone have science next?" I ask loudly into the room.

"I do," another kid says. I walk over to him. He's about my height with messy blonde hair that covers a large part of his face.

"You know how to get there?" I ask him.

"Yeah, it's in the same place as last year." He pulls a large bag onto his shoulder.

"Awesome, I'm gonna follow you, then."

"Uh, ok?"

I follow him out of the classroom. The hallway is filled with a bunch of kids coming out of the other rooms, everyone going towards the stairs to the tunnel. We follow the crowds down the stairs.

"So, what's your name?" I pull out the holo-recorder and turn it towards him.

"It's Joey." He looks at the holo-recorder. "What's that thing?"

"It's a holo-recorder. It lets me record videos on it," I explain.

He stares at it then looks back to me. "You said you're going to science. Do you know which one?"

"What do you mean which one?" I ask. He looks confused.

"What year are you?"

"First year," I say.

"Ah, then you're in the intro science class. I'll be in the secondary one next door," he explains.

"Can you still help me get there?" I ask.

"Yeah, we're still going to the same building."

We continue along the tunnels with the crowds of other students. I follow Joey down a new path, then up another set of stairs into a new building. He walks down the hallway a little and opens one of the nearby sliding doors.

"This one's your class," Joey says. As I step inside, I'm instantly transported back to University. The rows of desks and giant blackboard feel exactly like my dad's old classroom. I see Ava sitting at one of the far desks. Thank god there's a familiar face.

"I'm gonna go grab a seat." I wave thanks to Joey and walk towards the empty desks near Ava. I sit down and point the holo-recorder at her.

"So, tell me about yourself, Ava," I say, determined to break the ice with her.

"Who are you again?" Ava says.

"Olivia! I already told you that!" I remind her. We just had a whole class together.

"Right. What're you doing?"

"I'm recording everything."

"But why?"

"Well, my dad gave this thing to me. And he's busy with work so I thought I'd keep myself entertained."

"What's he do?" Ava asks.

"Oh, it's boring. He works over at War-denclyffe. Trying to invent some kind of new power system," I explain. It's tough to sum up exactly what his research is about.

"That sounds cool," Ava says.

"It's not," I say, trying to downplay my excitement about going to work with my dad on stuff. Then I remember what Kai told me about on my way into school. "Hey, have you ever been skating before?"

"No, what's that?" Ava asks.

"Oh, we're gonna have a lot of fun." I switch off the holo-recorder. "I learned about it earlier today before school. We should go together!"

"We?" Ava asks.

"Yeah! You and me. I don't wanna just go on my own so I thought you could come."

Ava looks carefully at me. "I guess…"

"Ok, so it's agreed, after school let's go together!" I say.

Before Ava can say anything more, a person who I assume is the teacher walks into the room and everyone gets really quiet. She walks up to the board and writes her name on it. Mrs. Barlowe.

"Hello, class. For those of you who do not yet know me, my name is Mrs. Barlowe." She wears a tightly-fit suit and a small pair of round glasses, and her grey hair is pulled back into a tight bun. "If you are here for freshman science, then you're in the right location. If that is not the class you're expecting, then you may be in the wrong place." She gives it a second, looking around the room at everyone. "Now, I'm sure you're all wondering what we're going to be learning about this year." She places a large box onto the table.

"What's that?" I whisper to Ava. Before she can answer my question, Mrs. Barlowe opens the box and removes a small plant in a clay pot. She places it on the table in front of the box.

"We're going to begin our curriculum with a look at plants indigenous to this city. And I'll be dividing you up into pairs for our first project." She begins walking around the room, pointing at pairs of people. "You two are together." She points at the first group. "And you two." She points at the two kids sitting behind us. "And lastly, the two of you will pair up for this project." She points at me and Ava. I look over at her and smile as Mrs. Barlowe walks back up to the front of the class.

"Looks like we'll be working together on this," I say.

"Sure does," she responds.

Mrs. Barlowe interrupts. "Ok, now that everyone's divided up into pairs, I'll explain the assignment to you." She lifts up the plant. "Everyone will be assigned one of the plants that grows around this city. You will then have to put together a short presentation about your assigned plant." She places the plant back onto the table. "And I expect each of you to do proper research." She walks around as she speaks.

"Sounds pretty fun," I say to Ava. She nods softly.

"And one more thing," Mrs. Barlowe continues, "I will give bonus points to any groups that manage to bring in a live specimen of their assigned plant." She pulls out a small bag from her desk drawer. "Everyone pull a slip out of the bag to find out what your assigned plant is." She begins to walk around the class.

I watch as she approaches each pair and everyone pulls out a small piece of parchment with writing on it. She eventually gets to us and holds the bag out in front of us. I excitedly reach in and pull out a piece of paper. Mrs. Barlowe walks back up to the front of the class.

"Ok, any questions?" She looks around.

"What'd we get?" Ava asks. I look down at the small slip of paper in my hand and the handwritten word scrawled across it.

"It says Edelweiss. Never heard of that," I say.

"Me either," Ava says.

"Ok good, if there's no more questions we can get on to our lesson for the day. And for your research I would recommend checking out the Botany section of either the June library or our school's library." She moves the plant from her desk over to the windowsill.

Over the next hour, she lectures about various parts of plants and their structure, drawing diagrams of leaves and stems on the chalkboard behind her as she talks. I look over at Ava. She's listening intently and copying down all the diagrams from the board into a small notebook with handwriting much neater than mine.

"Ok, I think we can wrap this up here today," Mrs. Barlowe says after a while of lecturing. "And you have a week to finish up your plant reports. Next week we'll begin presenting them to the rest of the class, ok?"

Everyone nods and there are murmurs of acknowledgment.

I start packing up all my stuff for the next class. "So where you off to next?"

"I've got music next," Ava says.

"Looks like we've got different schedules, then. I'm in English next." We walk out of the room together. I look down the hallway in both directions. "You don't by chance know how to get there, do you?"

"It's down that hallway, on the other side of school."

I remember back to my trouble finding the first class. "HEY! Anyone going to English next?" I shout into the hallway. I see another girl raise her hand. "Perfect, wait right there for me!" I yell to her before turning back to Ava. "And once classes are done meet me in front of school, ok? We'll go check out that ice skating."

"Sure," she says.

"Perfect! See you later." I smile and run over to the other girl and start walking with her to my next class.

I sit eagerly through my next classes, excited about the end of the day. In English we learn about famous authors and get a couple of reading assignments, and in astronomy we learn about the planets in our solar system. Feels silly since I learned most of that back in University when I was a kid. And finally, after astronomy, the day wraps up.

Luckily everyone seems to be going the same direction in the hallways this time. I follow the crowd and they lead me back to the main entrance of the school. Maybe if I'd been going here my whole life like them I'd be able to find my way around a little better, but honestly this whole school still feels like a maze. I can't imagine why anyone would've designed a school like this.

A cold breeze hits me the second I step outside. I shield my eyes from the brightness, pull my coat tight, and look around for Ava. I spot her standing near one of the large columns next to the doors.

"Hey! You waited for me!" I say.

"You told me to," she says.

"Yeah, I'm just glad you actually did." I laugh. "Let's go!" I start walking away from the school and Ava follows. We pass through the courtyard with the rest of the students, and from there everyone branches off in their own directions.

"Where is it?" Ava looks around.

"It's down the street a little ways. I saw them clearing off the ice earlier today." I point ahead. We keep walking until I eventually see some people in a crowd on the street ahead of us. "That must be where it is." I look down onto the ice shelf and see a crowd down there too.

"Is it really safe?" Ava asks.

"Well, look how many people are down there. It must be, right?"

"I suppose you're right," Ava agrees.

There are large wooden ladders leaning up against the edge of the street leading down to the ice shelf below, and a number of people are using them to climb down. I make sure my bag is securely on my shoulder then walk over to one of the ladders.

"Let's head down." I place my foot onto the top rung and start climbing. It's only about twenty feet down so it goes pretty quick. I reach the bottom and look back up to see Ava climbing down one of the other ladders, much slower and more cautiously than I had.

She eventually reaches the bottom and slowly walks over to me. The ice sheet feels weird. Unlike all the streets in town that have cobblestones beneath the snow, this is solid ice. Slippery and smooth.

"You know, I've heard if you distribute your weight from side-to-side while you walk, you're less likely to slip on the ice." We walk forward carefully together.

"Like a penguin," she says. I look over at her and she gives a small smile.

"Exactly," I say. The crowd on the ice stands around a large patch that looks like it's been polished completely flat, even smoother than the rest of the ice shelf. The snow has been packed into short walls around it and metal benches lean up against these makeshift walls. They actually look like the same benches from up on the street, probably lowered down onto the ice just for this event.

A bunch of people are sliding around on the ice, wearing weird shoes with metal blades on the bottom. Unlike my dad's ice shoes, which have a bunch of spikes, these just have the single blade along the bottom.

A woman walks up to us. "You two want to give it a try?"

"How do we do it?" I ask.

"Here, take these." She hands us large boots with the blades on the bottom. "These just slip on right over the shoes you already have on, then you can tighten them up with the straps here." She pulls one of the straps tighter and the boot closes itself tightly. I sit down on one of the nearby benches and pull the boots over my shoe. Ava sits down next to me.

"Seems simple enough." I pull the straps and feel the boot close around my foot. I stand up from the bench and immediately face plant into the ice shelf. Ava laughs. I think this is the first time I've actually heard her laugh. I feel myself blushing.

"Oh, honey, careful." The woman rushes over and helps me to my feet. "It takes a sec to get the hang of balancing on these," she explains. I hold onto her arm and practice taking small steps on the ice. "Look at that, you're getting better already." She stays close by but lets me practice getting the hang of walking.

"Can I help you up?" I walk over and ask Ava.

"I don't know, can you?" She smiles, then grabs my hand and pulls herself up off the bench. I manage to keep my balance. Once she's on her feet, she doesn't seem to have any issues staying upright.

"How are you so good at standing on these things?" I ask.

"I've got really good balance," she says. We walk over to the cleared patch of ice and step onto it together. With the blades underneath, I glide forward smoothly on the surface.

"This is pretty cool," I say, too soon. The second I've said it, I feel my balance go and I fall flat on my butt. Ava laughs again.

"Sorry for laughing," she says, still laughing.

"Laughing twice," I remind her.

"Yes, sorry for laughing twice," she says, sliding over and holding out her hand. I grab it and pull myself up. "You were just so eager to do this."

"It sounded fun," I say.

"I know. And you're right, it is fun." She glides ahead of me on the ice. I pull out the holo-recorder from my pocket and flip it on, following her as she glides around. It's kind of mesmerizing to watch. She glides back over.

"Come and join me." She pushes the recorder away and pulls my hands forward as she glides backwards. I can't believe she's never heard of this before. She pulls me along smoothly as I awkwardly try and keep my balance on the ice. We glide around until the sun begins to lower in the sky.

"Time to head back," someone nearby says loudly. Everyone on the ice makes their way off it. Ava and I walk back over to the bench and take the boots off, then someone comes around to collect them. The two of us walk over to the ladders and climb back up towards the street above.

"Which way are you?" Ava asks.

I look down both directions. "This way, I think." I point down one direction of the street, taking my best guess at the way home.

"You're not great with directions, are you?" she asks.

"No. But it's never stopped me before," I joke.

"Well, I'm the other direction." She pulls me in for a hug. "Today was fun. See you in class tomorrow?"

"Yeah, I'll see you in class," I say.

She waves as she walks off in the opposite direction. Back down on the ice, a group of androids have been enlisted to move all the benches back up to the street. What a fun day. I run back down the path towards my house.

CHAPTER FOUR

RESEARCH

"Hey, Dad," I call into the room.

He pops up from behind one of the large desks wearing a pair of ridiculously oversized goggles. "Hey, sweetie, what're you doing here?"

"Just showin' off some stuff for the recorder," I say, and he chuckles.

"And you wanted to record me?"

I walk closer and hold the holo-recorder up to his face. "Of course! You're the one who got this thing for me after all!" I laugh and he pushes it away. When I turn it off, he removes his goggles.

"So, you here to help out for a bit?" He gestures around to the mess of the room. "You know you don't have to give up your weekend if you don't want to."

"I know, I want to." I nod. "Oh, also, a girl from class is coming over to work on our science project with me."

"A science project?" Dad perks up when he hears this. "Anything I'd be able to help with?"

"You know anything about botany?"

"Not a thing," he says, "but who knows, there's probably some stuff in this place about it."

"You think?"

"Yeah, I'm sure one of the other caretakers must have been into botany. There's pretty much every kind of book somewhere here." He stands up from his spot behind the desk. "Wanna look with me?"

"Of course."

"Ok, good, come with me." He leads me up to the next level, which looks like it hasn't been touched since I was in here last week. There are still books stacked on the tables and even more filling every bookshelf around the room.

"Do you know where to look?" I ask.

"I'm afraid not. There's not really any organization to these shelves. It's just gonna take a bit of sorting through." He starts pulling out books from the shelf. "At some point, I'd like to go back and reorganize this whole floor." He stacks the books onto the table next to him.

I start to wander through the bookshelves and examine what's in all the stacks. I didn't really look too closely the last time I was here. There's a mix of books, some almost new, others ancient. Thick volumes with old leather covers, so worn down you can't make out the titles anymore.

"How long have all of these been here?" I pull out one of the really old ones from the shelf. It's pretty thin and, like many of the others, whatever text used to be on the cover has long since faded.

"Hard to say. But if I had to guess I'd say there are probably some that've been here since the lighthouse was built."

I look over the book in my hand. Since the lighthouse was built, huh? I gently open the book. The pages feel brittle and old and the text is almost completely faded but I manage to make out some of the words on the title page, *A Midsummer Night's Dream*.

"Oh, I know this one," I say. As I hold it up, a small piece of folded-up paper falls from between the pages. The paper is a deep shade of blue with a bunch of white lines scribbled on the corner I can see.

"Really?"

I pass him the book as he comes over. "It's Shakespeare!"

He flips through the pages, revealing some faded but beautiful illustrations. "Well, what do you know? That's a pretty cool find." He hands the book carefully back to me and I gently close it before sliding it back onto the shelf. The two of us pore over the shelves together, looking for anything plant-related, with Dad occasionally pulling books out and placing them onto the nearby desks.

"Oh, I think I found one," I say, pulling a book off the shelf.

"Which one?"

"It's called *Astrobotany*! That should be helpful, right?"

"Well, unless your plants are growing in outer space, I'm not sure this is what you need." He chuckles. "But I'm going to add it to the pile anyways. At least this way we can still put it into our new botany section when we start to get this mess organized." He places the book onto the desk with the others and I look at the pile.

We've managed to create a nice little collection of botany-related books. I read through some of the titles: *Desert Flora, Cooking With Seaweed, Rural Farming Guide, Plant Genetics*, and of course the *Astrobotany* book I found.

"When's your project due?" he asks.

"On Monday," I say. "We're gonna present it to the class."

"That should be fun."

"I hope so. I told Ava to come over today so we could work on it and get it ready for Monday."

"So Ava's your friend?"

"Yeah, she's the one I showed you in the holo-recordings," I say.

"Oh yeah, the girl in the funny outfit, right?"

"Yup! That's her."

"Well, I can't wait to finally meet her."

"Why?" I ask.

"You've been talking about her all week."

My face turns red. "Not that much…" I say softly.

"It's ok, I won't embarrass you," he says, but somehow I don't believe him.

We keep looking through the shelves and my eyes catch sight of a familiar title, *The Grid: a Modern-Day Power System*. I hand the book to my dad. "Do you need this one?" I've heard him mention the grid a couple of times with his work.

"Where'd you find this?"

"Just over on the shelf," I say. He's already busy flipping through the pages.

"I'll be back in a little bit, I just want to skim though this," he says, his nose already fully in the book. I'll be lucky if I see him again before dinner. He walks back over to the stairs and down to the first level of the lighthouse, leaving me to search for books on my own.

I spend a couple more minutes searching and manage to find a pretty decent number of books about plants. No idea if any will actually have what we need, though. I notice the folded-up piece of paper that had fallen out of the book earlier still laying on the floor nearby. I lean down to pick it up but as I'm about to unfold it, I hear a knocking echoing up from the floor below.

"Hey, Olive, I think that's for you," my dad calls up.

I tuck the paper into my pocket and run downstairs to the front door. As I pull open the large metal door, Ava is standing there with a bag over her shoulder.

"Good to see you." I give her a hug as she steps inside and I let the door swing shut behind her. Her face lights up with wonder as she takes in the room.

"It's not at all what I imagined," she says, looking around with wide eyes.

"What did you imagine?" I ask, as she takes off her coat and I hang it next to the door.

"I don't know. I always used to wonder what was in this building. There's a lot more stuff than I was expecting."

"We're working on that," my dad says, walking over to us, still holding the book I had given him.

"I–I didn't mean..." she stutters.

He looks around the room. "Oh no, it's fine. This place is a complete mess, but this one's not my fault so I don't feel as bad about it." He chuckles and Ava laughs nervously.

"Let me show you what I found," I say, pulling her up the staircase to the next level.

"You two let me know if you need anything," Dad says. I feel my face getting red from embarrassment. I knew he was gonna say something like that. We reach the next level and Ava looks around again.

"This is the library level." I gesture to all the books.

"There's so many books," she says.

"Yeah, and I pulled out a few that might be able to help us." I lead her over to the table where I had put all the books about plants.

"Wow, you found a lot!" She picks up one of them and looks it over.

"I thought we could go though some here and if we don't find anything we can check out the library."

"Sounds good to me," she says.

"Ok, follow me." I grab some books myself and gesture for her to do the same, then we climb the stairs, each with an armful of plant books. When we reach the top floor, I place the books onto the ground.

"What is this place?" she asks, carefully stacking her books next to mine.

"It's the top floor of the lighthouse."

"I mean, I can tell that. But what's with all the statues?" She walks up to the closest

figure and examines it closely. "Like, why does it say 'Mercury' here?" She reads off the plaque at the base of the statue.

"Not really sure. I think they're just here for decoration." I walk over to the large seat in the middle of the room and sit down. "But this is my favorite part by far."

She follows me over and looks at the chair. "Weird place for a chair."

"Yeah, but it's got a great view." I point out the window, but her attention seems stuck on all the statues. "So you wanna get started with the research?" This snaps her back.

"That's probably a good idea."

The two of us sprawl out on the floor next to the pile of books and I pass one over to her before grabbing one for myself. We each leaf through the pages, looking for any information about the edelweiss plant. I come to a section and read through the list of plants in the book, but edelweiss isn't listed.

"No luck in this one," I say, swapping the book for another on the pile.

She closes hers too. "Same with this one." She drops it onto the pile next to mine. "Most of these are about totally different regions." She holds up the *Astrobotany* book. "Or outer space?" She stares at me closely.

"Ok, I'll admit that one was a bit of a long shot."

"Astrobotany sounds like something out of science fiction."

I laugh and open up the next book. The room is starting to feel like an oven with all the sunlight shining through the windows, the once-cold stone floor now warmed by the heat of the sun. We spend about an hour looking through the pile of books with very little luck.

She places the last book back onto the pile. "It looks like we're out of luck with any of these. Do you think the school library would have any?"

"Let's try the June library first," I say.

"Why there? It's kind of old and dusty. You really think they'd have what we need?"

"They've got a lot of stuff! Plus, I have another book I have to bring back," I say.

We both get up and walk down the stairs back to the first floor. I grab Ava's coat and hand it to her, then grab mine from one of the other pegs and pull it on.

On the other side of the room, my dad looks up from his book. "You two going out?"

"Yeah, we're gonna run to the library and see if they have any more books on plants," I say.

"Good luck. I'll see you at home later! Nice to finally meet you, Ava," he says, returning to his book.

We step outside, back into the cold, and follow the winding path into town. The weekends seem to be a lot busier than other times. Even out here we pass a couple of other people out walking around. Down below us I can see a bunch of busses parked at the docks and further out on the ice shelf, another one kicks up a flurry of snow as it crawls away from June.

We reach the main part of the city and start climbing the streets up towards the library. We make awkward small talk until we arrive and head inside. I lead Ava over to the desk where Astrid sits.

"Hey, Astrid, I brought this back for you." I take the book about androids out of my bag and hand it over to her.

"Thanks for bringing it back. Find what you were looking for?" she asks.

"Not quite. Still an interesting read though," I say.

"Well, I do have something else for you. I found out when that painting is from," she says.

"Oh really? That's amazing!" I think back to the old painting tucked away in the back hallway of the library.

"I thought you'd be excited. It was painted back in 2287, and from what I could find, the people in front of the building are the crew of a ship called the *Phoebe*. But so far that's all I was able to find on it."

"That's so cool!" I say. I turn to Ava. "I'll show it to you once we're done with our project."

This catches Astrid's attention. "What's the project?" she asks.

"We're researching plants that grow around June," I explain. "Actually, would you be able to show us where all the books on plants are?"

"Of course. You must be in Mrs. Barlowe's science class, right?" She gets up from her desk and leads us into the stacks of bookshelves.

"How did you know?" I ask.

"I remember doing the same project for her class when I was your age." Ava and I follow her to a section that says BOTANY on a small metal plaque. "You should be able to find what you're looking for somewhere in here." She points to a section of books.

"Thank you," Ava says to her.

"Sure thing, sweetie. You two just let me know if you need anything else, ok?"

"We will!" I say. Astrid walks back over to her desk and I start looking through the books on the shelf with Ava. Finally, a promising one catches my eye. I pull it off the shelf. *Cold-Weather Plants*.

"What's that one?" Ava asks.

"It's a book on cold-weather plants. Let's take a look through it." I lead her down the shelves to the smaller atrium where we grab a seat in two of the large comfy chairs. We lay the book across the arms of the chair and flip through it together. There are dozens of photos of plants growing in the snow and on the tops of mountains. Finally, we reach a page that says EDELWEISS right at the top.

"That's it!" she says loudly. A couple of people turn to look at us. "Sorry…" she says to them.

There's a photo of the plant on the page, an almost fuzzy-looking white flower.

"So, it's like a flower?" I say.

"Seems to be," Ava says. Another image shows bunches of this white flower growing around short grass.

"It's pretty."

"It really is," Ava agrees. "It says it mostly grows at really high altitudes."

That's when a thought occurs to me. "Do you think we could find one growing somewhere around here?"

She looks confused. "What do you mean?"

"Mrs. Barlowe said if we bring one in, we get extra credit!"

"Yeah, but I don't think anyone's actually gonna do that," she says.

"But wouldn't it be fun? We could go look around town for one!"

"But what about the actual report?" Ava says.

"We'll write that tomorrow. We have until Monday, after all." I shut the book. "Let's check this out then we can go on an adventure to find one!"

I run up to Astrid with the book and place it on the table in front of her. Ava catches up behind me. "We'd like to take this one out please," I say.

"Of course, good choice." She neatly writes the name of the book into the big ledger on her desk before passing it back over to me. "Good luck with the project."

"Thank you," Ava says. We wave good-bye to her and leave the library.

"Here, put this in your bag." I hand the book over to Ava and she tucks it away.

"Where do we even begin to look?" she asks.

"Well, it says it grows in high elevation, right? Let's start up there." I turn and look up towards the top streets of June. The stone steps stretch up far above us. Ava follows me as we start to climb them. After about fifteen minutes, we reach the top street, both slightly out of breath.

There's a large wooden sign at the top that says NOW LEAVING JUNE. Beyond it lies a flat white landscape, almost exactly like the ice shelf below the city except that this one has a number of small bushes and shrubs growing throughout it.

"What's out that way?" I ask.

"Not too much, it's mostly traders that go past here."

We follow the top street along the edge of the city. It curves around the rim of June, looking down over the entire town. The street is lined with small benches nestled up against a short wooden fence that separates the street from the white tundra beyond. There are some plants growing along the side of the road but none of them look like the one we're searching for.

"Are there more cities further north?" I ask as we continue along the street.

"Not that I know of. I think it's mostly small villages," she explains.

"I can't imagine living so far outside of the city," I say.

"I think the people living out that way have been doing it for centuries. They're probably used to it by now."

I try to imagine what the villages must look like but nothing comes to mind. "I can't even picture that," I say. "I'm still getting used to June. It's much bigger than University."

"You keep mentioning that. What is University?" She leans down to look at some of the plants growing near one of the benches.

"What do you mean? It's University!" I say.

"Is that a city?" she asks and I don't know how to respond to that.

"Of course it is! I can't believe you've never heard of it!"

"I've never been outside of June," she says.

"Really? Why not?"

"Just never really came up, I guess. My whole life is here." She stands up again and we keep walking.

"Well, it's pretty far from here." I look out over June. "It's about a three-day bus ride across the ice shelf, then four more days beyond that by trolley," I explain.

"I can't even imagine going that far," she says.

"I'd never gone this far before moving. Only small trips. And never anywhere this cold." I pull my coat closer.

"Wait, really?" She looks over at me.

"Yeah it's never been this cold in University. No ice in sight, except when the ice deliveries come around," I say.

"What's University like?"

"Well, it's a bit warmer than here," I joke.

"Not hard to be."

"It started out as a small school, then a collection of schools, and they just kept adding to it until it had become as big as a city. Now people travel from all over to study there."

"Wow, that sounds amazing. Have you always lived there?"

"Yeah, Dad's been a teacher there my whole life."

"Do you miss it?"

I think about that for the first time since leaving. "Yeah. I like new places, but I do still miss all my friends."

"Yeah, that must be tough. At least you're already making some new friends here." She gives me a big smile.

I give a little smile, despite the feeling of homesickness that's come over me. Then I notice a small patch of white flowers. "Hey, look at these." I pull Ava over and we lean down together as she pulls the book out from her bag, opening it to the section about the edelweiss flower.

"Ah, too bad, they're white but that's definitely not the same flower," I say with disappointment.

"Oh wait! I have an idea!" Ava says suddenly. "Let's go check out the flower shop!"

"Isn't it kind of cheating to get it from a shop?" I joke.

"I didn't mean to get it there! I just thought they might have a better idea where we might be able to find one growing."

"Oh, that is a good idea. You know where it is?" I ask.

"Of course I do. You forget, I'm the one who actually knows how to get around here," she teases.

The climb back down the stairs is much easier than the one going up. I feel like after living here for a while I'm gonna have super strong leg muscles.

"It's over this way," Ava says, turning onto one of the streets. I follow her until we stop in front of a large building. It looks like a completely different flower shop than the one my dad had brought me to. Unlike the other one, this shop has way more windows. It looks like the entire roof is made from glass. The building sticks out like a sore thumb.

"Lot of windows," I notice.

"You'll see why." Ava leads me inside. The room is filled floor-to-ceiling with plants, and the light shining through all the windows heats up the room so it feels almost like summer back home, or the top floor of the lighthouse. A thick floral scent wafts around us as Ava walks up to the shopkeeper.

"Excuse me, can we ask you a question?"

"Of course. What can I help you with?" The shopkeeper wears a floral summer dress with a dirty apron over it and large straw hat. The apron has a bunch of gardening tools stuck into various pockets.

"Do you know where we can find a plant like this?" Ava holds up the book and the shopkeeper leans in closely to look at the page.

"Oh, that's an edelweiss flower, isn't it?"

"Yeah, it's for a school project," Ava explains.

"I'm afraid I don't have any in the shop," she says.

I pace around as the two of them talk. The floors here look like they've just been carved into the natural dirt and churned up until they were soft enough to plant in, a harsh contrast between the frozen dirt and stone streets in the rest of town. Throughout the dirt floors are small, uneven brick walls separating the beds of different plants from the paths throughout the shop.

"Do you know where we might be able to find one?" I ask, joining the conversation.

"Well, I know they grow in super high areas," she begins, halfway lost in thought before suddenly snapping out of it. "I think the only place I ever remember seeing them was on the cliffside south of June," she says, before catching herself and adding, "but I wouldn't recommend climbing up that way.

They don't keep it up the way they used to. Plus, most of it is off-limits now," she warns.

"Thanks for letting us know anyways," Ava says. She closes the book and puts it back into her bag. We leave the shop again. "I can still smell the flowers."

"So, you want to go check out the cliffs?" I ask.

"What? Weren't you just listening to her?"

"Of course I was! She just told us where we could find it!"

"Did you miss the part where she said it was dangerous and restricted?" she argues.

"That's never stopped me before." I give her a small smile.

There's a pause before she speaks again. "Fine. As long as we're careful," she says.

"Do you know how to get there?"

"You see those cliffs over there?" She points to the towering cliff face that stretches up alongside the south side of the city.

"Oh, I could've probably found that one," I say, and she laughs.

"With your sense of direction, I'm not sure you would have," she teases.

"Hey, I'm not that bad!" I say, and she laughs again. We start walking in the direction of the cliff face, climbing down the steps until we reach the first street level. "They're pretty tall," I say.

"Not too late to turn back." Ava looks over at me. "There's still time to go back and just write our report like normal."

"No, we're going on an adventure." I continue towards the cliff until we reach the base. "Have you ever been up this way?"

"We did a couple of field trips when I was a kid, but it's been a few years," she says, looking up at the cliff with me.

"Do you know how we can get up there?" I look around as we get closer to the base.

"Yeah, there's a trail over here we can start at." She leads me over to the entrance of a small trail marked with a large wooden post. The post is painted dark blue and has an arrow pointing steeply up the rocks where the small trail seems to lead.

We follow it up the front of the cliffs, searching the clumps of small plants and occasional shrubs growing out of the rocks for the edelweiss flower. Unlike the rest of June, there's very little snow over here. Just a light dusting along the ground. If I had to guess, I'd say the amount of wind on these cliffs probably keeps most of it off. Even with my coat I can still feel the breeze blowing through me.

The path zig-zags back and forth as it climbs. Every couple of feet is another one of the large blue posts pointing upwards along the path.

"I thought the steps in June were a lot," I say to Ava, a little out of breath.

"We can always turn back if you don't want to keep going," she says. Unlike me, she's not out of breath.

"You wish," I wheeze. I keep following her until I see a small patch of white flowers. "Wait, over there." I point, and Ava and I run over to check them out.

"It's a different flower," she says, bending down to pick one up. "But still pretty." She tucks the flowers into her bag anyways.

"Agreed." I'm a little disappointed but we keep climbing up the path. Luckily Ava seems to know exactly where she's going. We're up pretty high now; the only thing separating us from the edge of the rocks is a small rope fence, just about waist height, strung through a series of metal posts. Not the biggest comfort, I've got to admit.

"You said they used to bring you on field trips up here?" I ask.

"Yeah, all the time. There's an outlook a little further up." She keeps climbing as I struggle a little to keep up with her. After about an hour, we come to a small, flat area with rusted old benches bolted into the rock. From up here I can see out over the entire city, even the lighthouse far on the opposite side of June.

"Everything looks so small from up here." I look down at the buildings below us.

"Yeah, it's wild how high this goes," she says.

I scan the streets, trying to make out any details, but it's almost impossible from up here. I pull out the holo-recorder and pan over the city with it. I keep turning until Ava's in the picture. She notices me recording her and I quickly turn it off.

"So how about those flowers?" I say, looking around. There are some small patches of plants around.

"I'm not seeing any that look like the edelweiss." She looks around at some of the plants near me until I notice another path continuing up the rocks nearby.

"What about further up? You think we'll find anything up there?" I ask her. She shakes her head.

"It's not safe to climb up that far," she says.

"What do you mean? We've already come all this way! What's a little further?" I start walking towards the other path.

She grabs my arm. "It's restricted, though."

"Ok, fine, in that case we'll only stay up there for a little." I give her a wink then pull away and start climbing up the path. She runs after me.

"Fine, but if we get in trouble, it's your fault," she says, catching up to me.

This area is much steeper, and narrower too. Unlike climbing up the face of the cliff, this path goes directly between two large boulders and is a lot rockier. I squeeze through and try to keep my balance on the weird footing.

Suddenly it looks like I've reached the end of the path until I look up at the wall in front of me. There are old-looking metal pipes sunk deep into the rock leading up, like a makeshift ladder. I reach out and pull on one of the pieces of metal. Luckily it seems to be secure.

"You can't seriously be considering climbing that, are you?" Ava asks with disbelief.

"Oh, come on, aren't you the least bit curious what's up there?" I plead.

"Do you really think we're going to find the flower up there?" she asks, crossing her arms.

"It's not about that anymore. This adventure is taking us in a new direction! You have to be willing to go with the flow a little bit!" I step up onto the first rung and it doesn't budge. I climb up a few more rungs then turn back and smile at Ava. "So, you coming?"

"You're gonna get us in big trouble with an attitude like that," she says, begrudgingly climbing up after me.

The rock starts to slant forwards as we climb, until I'm almost crawling along the rock face. I can see what looks like the top a couple of feet above me. I grab the last rungs and pull myself forwards.

When I reach the top, I see something I didn't expect at all. Stretching out before me is a vast crater filled with hundreds of colorful flowers and a massive tree sitting right in the middle.

"No way," I say.

"What is it?" Ava asks.

"You just gotta see this." I climb over the rim of the crater and slide down into the center. Not only are there plants everywhere, but the whole area is completely warm. Not a trace left of the cold breeze I felt only moments before.

"What is that?" I see Ava's head pop up from the rim of the crater, a look of shock on her face.

"Can you believe we almost turned back?"

"How is this possible?" She climbs over the edge of the stone and slides down next to me. I reach out and help guide her down. Her hand feels soft in mine.

"Got me beat," I say. "It's your town after all." I give her a playful nudge. She walks around and looks at all the plants.

"Is that a willow tree?" She stares up at the tree before us.

"Maybe? I'm not really sure," I say. It is impressive, though. And old, too. Sometimes you can just feel it by looking at trees that they've been there for ages.

There's a small path of stones leading up to the massive tree, each one cracked by grass growing up between it. The branches of the tree hang down in front of us like a massive curtain, their ends dragging back and forth over the ground as they sway. I push them aside and step through into a new world of twisted branches and a soft flooring of thick grass. Ava lays down in the grass.

"It's so warm," she says.

"Must be why all the plants are growing here," I say. Although it's mostly just grass under the tree, with only a few clumps of flowers.

"I've never been in a place this warm before." She runs her fingers through the grass.

"Not even in the summer?" I lay down in the grass and stare up at the sun filtering through the branches.

"Nah, it's frozen pretty much the whole year round." She pauses. "Thanks for dragging me along." She reaches out and grabs my hand. I don't know what to say. My stomach has so many butterflies I can barely speak.

"No prob," I say awkwardly. 'No prob?' I couldn't have said anything other than that? I turn my head and look towards her. Our eyes meet.

"Well, would you look at that," she says, reaching out her other hand behind my head. As she pulls her hand back, I notice the white flower in her grip.

"Is that the edelweiss?" I ask.

"Looks like your crazy adventure worked out after all." She looks at the flower closely before handing it to me. I take the edelweiss from her, although I have to admit there's not a single part of me that's thinking about the flower anymore.

CHAPTER FIVE

THE SEA CAVES

I follow my dad down the path to Warden-clyffe, still in a sleepy haze. The sun is still rising over the city and the streets are nearly empty. Just a few random people walking around.

"Why do you think they're up so early?" I ask, looking at some of the various people we pass by.

"They're probably up to run the shops," he explains.

"But this early?" I ask.

"Well, there's a lot of prep that needs to happen before opening. Plus, look down there." He turns me towards the docks.

"Are those busses?" I ask. It's hard to tell from this far away.

"Yeah, those are some of the traders. There's a bunch of them that pass through super early in the day on their way to other trade ports."

I look at some of the people on the street again. The patterns in their clothing are much more colorful than what I'm used to seeing people up here wearing. One has a large, beaded necklace hanging over their coat. Another wears a big knit hat with a pattern that matches their shawl.

Accompanying the various traders are a number of androids, many of whom are carrying large wooden crates. Each one seems to follow one of the people and some look like they have patterns etched into their metal. Are they really just used to carry stuff around here? I can't imagine doing the same thing every day like that.

My dad and I reach the lighthouse and go inside. I take off my coat and hang it near the door. He throws his over one of the nearby chairs.

"So, what're we working on today?" I ask.

"You up for taking down some walls?" he asks.

"Of course." I nod excitedly.

"Ok, good, come with me." He leads me up to the fourth floor and over to one of the walls which has a thin wood paneling covering it. He hands me a small crowbar.

"What's this for?" I ask.

"I need all the wood paneling removed so I can get to the wires." He grabs another crowbar from the table for himself.

"Awesome." I dig the crowbar in between two of the panels and lean against it. The wood creaks under my weight until it finally splinters and cracks apart, revealing the mess of wires behind. They run all the way up the wall into the ceiling above, just like all the floors below.

"What're all these wires for?" I ask, pulling at some of them.

"Careful with those." My dad reaches out and pulls my hand back from the wires. "They're all part of the old equipment from Wardenclyffe. It's connected back to the gird," he explains.

"So? Isn't everything?" I get back to work pulling off the panels.

"Yeah, but that's kind of the problem," he says.

"Why's that a problem?" I ask. He stops prying up the panels.

"Well, right now pretty much everything relies on the grid for power. Everything from the trolley systems to the kettle in our kitchen," he says.

"Yeah, it's been that way for ages though. What's the problem?" I keep working on pulling up the panels as he explains; there's something super fun about snapping them in half.

"What happens when the grid stops working?" he asks, and I stop working.

"Is it going to?"

"That's just it, no one knows. There's very little information about how it works. And as far as we know, no one's been maintaining the systems for over a century. It's just been running on its own." He starts pulling up some of the panels again and I do the same.

"But what's the lighthouse got to do with any of that?"

"Well, the lighthouse is one of the oldest structures that's connected to the grid. I'm hoping to study it and maybe understand more about how the grid works."

"But why?"

"That's the whole point of my research here. I'm hoping if I can learn how the grid works, I can use that same technology to create some kind of new power system. That way, if the grid ever fails, the world wouldn't be without power." He looks around the room. "But if I'm ever going to do that, I need to understand how it works first."

"Yeah, I remember you telling me about the power cell part. So, why're we tearing all these panels off?" I ask, tossing some of the wood scraps into a small pile.

"If I do manage to develop some new power cell, I also need some kind of way to distribute the power to everywhere, that's why we also need some kind of new power system. I think there might be something in this tower that would work for that," he explains.

"Why do you think that?"

"Well, there are rumors that this place was built to send out powerful radio signals. And I have a theory it might be possible to send out power using the same system."

"Sounds like a lot of work," I say. He chuckles.

"Yeah, well, it'll probably take decades. And there's no guarantee anything will come from it," he says. "Plus, for all I know the grid might actually last forever."

"That would be good, right?" I ask.

"Oh, of course, it would just mean there wouldn't really be a need for any of the work I'm doing now." He laughs. "And the system really only works if I have some kind of power to actually distribute through it."

"I know you'll figure it out," I say. I notice the clock on the wall. "Oh no, it's almost time for class."

"Come here." He pulls me in for a big hug. "I'll see you at home for dinner, right?"

"I actually might have some plans for dinner already." I give him a big hug back.

"No problem. Tell Ava I say hi." He smiles at me.

"I will," I say, my face red with embarrassment. I quickly run back down the stairs, grab my coat and my schoolbag, and leave the lighthouse. As I step outside and my eyes adjust to the brightness, I catch a flash of red out of the corner of my eye. I turn and see the woman in the red coat disappear behind a corner.

I peer out from behind the lighthouse, careful so she won't see me watching her. Why's she sneaking around out this way? There's nothing out past the lighthouse, right? At least not on any of the maps I've looked at. She moves quickly across the snow and stops in front of some of the rocks. She places her hand on them before seeming to disappear behind them completely.

My gut tells me to follow her, but last time I did that I almost didn't make it to school. I think better of it and run off in the opposite direction, towards school instead. But I'm definitely coming back later to check out what's out there. Maybe I'll even bring Ava along.

I get to school and look up at the large clock on the front of the building. Early, good. I wanna make sure I'm ready for this presentation today. I run down the hallways towards the science classroom. I liked when art was the first class of the day but our classes rotate so it won't happen again for a few days.

I slide open the door to the classroom and find it completely empty. I step inside and close the door behind me, then walk over to my desk and sit down. Usually, Ava gets here before me, so I think she'll be surprised to see me this early. I take the holo-recorder out of my pocket and start recording, determined to document her reaction. I wait quietly for a few minutes until the door finally slides open and Ava walks in.

"You know, the whole recording thing was cute at first, but now it's getting a little old," Ava says. She does look surprised to see me though. "And since when are you on time for class?" she teases as she sits down next to me.

"You're not gonna say that when we look back at these recordings years from now," I say.

"I highly doubt that," Ava says. "What've you been up to today?"

"Just helping my dad out in the lab."

"Oh yeah? Doing anything fun?"

"Nah, just boring stuff. He's still working on that power cell." I lean in closer with the recorder and get obnoxiously close.

"And what would that be? You know, for those of us who might not have been listening the other day?"

The holo-recorder beeps. Maybe I shouldn't have used up all the recording time waiting for her. I turn it off.

"Oh, you know all about it," I say. "Remember? During art class last week? I talked about how that's what he started working on in University." I catch her smiling at me and pause. "You're teasing me," I say.

"Why yes, I am." She rests her head onto her hand. "How could I forget about it? You talked for like an hour straight." She smiles again.

"Well get ready for another exciting adventure." I smile back at her as the door opens and a couple other kids walk into the room.

"Oh yeah? What've you got for us this time?"

"There's this woman I've seen around town in a red coat," I begin.

"Oh yeah, I've seen her around too," she says, cutting me off.

"Wait really?" I say loudly. A couple of other kids in the room turn to look. "What do you know about her?" I lean in closer and lower my voice a little.

"Not much. I mean, she's just kind of around. But there aren't too many others in a red coat." She laughs.

"Well, I've been following her, and I think she's up to something," I say.

"Oh yeah? She's 'up to something'?" Ava makes air quotes with her fingers.

"I'm serious. Before my first day of school, I caught her inside one of the buildings in the old district," I explain.

"That's weird. There's nothing over there, right?" she asks, and I shake my head.

"But that's not the weird part. I caught her stealing one of the power cells out of an android," I say quietly.

"Why would she do that?" She lowers her voice too.

"I don't know. But this morning on my way here, I caught her heading up to the rocks north of the lighthouse."

Almost the entire class has arrived by now.

"Why? What's up there? I thought it was just some caves."

"No idea. Caves would be cool to explore. But either way, you and me are going to check it out after class to find out for sure," I say. Before Ava can object to my plan, the door opens and Mrs. Barlowe walks in. Her suit today is a dark purple with grey trim.

"Seats please, everyone." All the other students walk over to their desks and quietly sit down. She places her bag onto the desk. "Ok, you all have had a week to work on your research projects and today each group will present their project to the rest of the class. Any volunteers?" She looks around the room. All the other kids skillfully avoid her gaze.

I raise my hand high. "We'll go first!"

"Wait, really?" Ava leans in and whispers.

"Olivia and Ava will present first then." Mrs. Barlowe walks over to her desk and sits down.

"Yeah, come on! Ours is way better than everyone else's," I whisper to Ava as I stand up and pull her to the front of the classroom with me.

"So, remind us all again what your assigned plant was?" Mrs. Barlowe asks.

"The edelweiss flower," I say.

"Ok, go ahead and tell us about it." Mrs. Barlowe pulls out a small clipboard with paper on it and a pencil. She takes notes while occasionally looking up at us.

"Well, the edelweiss tends to grow at very high altitudes, usually in pretty rocky areas." I give Ava a smile, thinking back to our climb up to find one. "It's a pretty white flower and looks kind of fuzzy," I explain.

"It's in the same category as other flowers like the daisy and thistle," Ava continues. "It's even been used in some types of medicines." We seem to be losing the interest of the rest of the class, but that somehow takes a little bit of the pressure off.

"And the most exciting part is this." I run over to my bag and pull out the edelweiss flower we found this weekend. It's a little crushed from being in my bag but still clearly an edelweiss. This seems to perk everyone up a little bit as they look at the flower.

"May I see that?" Mrs. Barlowe asks. I walk over and hand her the flower. She looks at it closely. "I haven't seen one of these in years. Where did you find this?"

"We found it growing high up," I say, burying the lede.

"I can't believe you actually found one," she says, lifting it up to her nose and smelling it. I remember how sweet it smelled when we first found it.

"Well, you said we'd get bonus points if we brought the plant, right?" I remind her.

"Yes, I suppose I did say that." She seems mesmerized by the flower. Then she looks up at us. "May I hold onto this?"

"Of course," I say.

"Thank you. Please continue." She returns to her clipboard.

"Unfortunately, the flower is hard to cultivate and doesn't grow easily in a lot of climates. But it also has a slightly sweet smell to it," Ava says.

"Can we smell it?" one of the kids in the class asks.

"Sure, pass this around carefully." Mrs. Barlowe hands the flower to me and I pass it around the class. Each person takes a turn smelling the flower before returning it to me, and I hand it back to Mrs. Barlowe. We give a couple more facts about the flower, the class now fully listening to what we have to say.

"Any questions?" Ava asks as we wrap up our presentation. There are a couple of murmurs from the kids, but no one responds.

"Thank you, you two," Mrs. Barlowe says. Ava and I walk back over to our seats and sit back down. "Who's next?" she asks. No one responds so she calls on one of the other pairs. We spend the rest of the class watching other kids present their plants to the class and talk about where they grow, and what they're used for. It seems like Ava and I are the only two who brought the actual flower.

The class ends and Ava and I gather our things. We walk through the tunnels of the school over to our next class in the art building.

"Ok, so we've got a couple more classes, then you'll meet me in front of the school, right?" I ask her.

She nods. "Fine, I'll come meet you there."

"It'll be fun!" I say, trying to convince her.

"It better be," she says.

"Just look how well our last adventure went," I say.

"Fair point." She smiles at me as we walk into the art class together. Only a few more hours until we're free.

After my last class, I rush back to the front entrance of the school and watch the crowds as I wait for Ava, although after a few minutes I begin to worry that she skipped out on me. Just as I'm wondering if I was too pushy this time, I feel someone's hand grab mine.

"You wait long?" a voice asks in my ear, and I nearly jump and pull my hand away. I turn and see Ava. "What was that reaction?" she asks.

"You just startled me. I was a little lost in thought," I say. I feel bad now that I pulled my hand away from hers.

"You wanna head out?"

"Yeah, let's go!" I pull out the holo-recorder and point it at her as we walk.

"So where are we off to today?" Ava says jokingly.

"We're going to explore some caves," I say, playing along with her.

"And why are we doing that?" Ava asks. She sounds like an actor.

"Because it's exciting!" I do my best impression of an actress I like. "Why wouldn't you be excited about that?"

"Because you're dragging me along on another one of your 'adventures'." She breaks out of the voice and does air quotes sarcastically.

"Oh, come on, don't be sour! It's gonna be a lot of fun!" I plead with her and turn off the holo-recorder. "Here, I'll even leave this off. Today can just be about exploring," I say.

We reach the other side of the school courtyard and walk up the steps towards one of the higher streets.

"So, what do you think she's up to?" Ava asks.

"I don't know, but it has to be something involving the androids, right?"

"Do you think it's anything illegal?"

Ava makes a good point.

"If it is, that's all the more reason for us to do something about it," I say. "And you're sure you don't know anything else about her?"

"I mean, she's just always been around. I've never really thought too much about her."

"What do you mean always?" I ask. We turn onto the street and walk along the path towards the lighthouse.

"I mean she's been around for years. As far back as I can remember."

I remember back to when I met her on my first day here in June. "But she arrived on the same bus as I did when we moved up here."

"Yeah, sometimes she's gone for, like, months at a time. I'll just stop seeing her then suddenly she'll be back around town again. I just assumed she traveled a lot," Ava says as we pass by the lighthouse, continuing down the path towards the rocky cliffs.

"Everything I learn about her just raises more questions."

The path gets much rockier as we go. It's the same black rock as the cliffs we climbed on the other side of June, although these aren't nearly as tall and towering. I lead us to where I saw the woman earlier today.

"She was over here?" Ava looks around at the rocks.

"Yeah, and then she disappeared up past there." I point ahead. We come to the edge of the rocks and turn a corner, right where I saw the woman vanish from my view, and find a series of caves carved into the rocks.

"There's so many of them," Ava says, looking at all the caves.

"Which one do you think she went in?" I ask.

"I know exactly which one she went into."

"How can you possibly know that?" I look over at her and she's got a big smile on her face.

"You're not much of a detective, are you?" she teases.

"Oh, come on, just tell me." She points down at a trail of footprints in the snow. "Wait, are those…?"

"We can literally just follow her trail," Ava says.

"I can't believe I missed that." I shake it off. "Come along then." I run along the trail of footprints towards one of the smaller cave entrances. The wind stops blowing my hair around as I step over the threshold. Ava stands next to me, the only light coming from the cave entrance behind us. We stare into the darkness together.

"How are we going to explore this without any light?" she asks. It's a good point.

"Well, there's some light, we can see a little bit ahead," I say, walking forward a little bit. There are a couple of small rocks on the ground but apart from that I don't see anything interesting. I put my hands in front of me and slowly keep walking forward until my foot hits something that makes a loud metal clang. I stop suddenly.

"What was that?" Ava asks from a little behind me.

"Sounds like there's something metal on the floor." I tap the ground with my foot and the metal sound echoes through the cave. "Yeah, it's definitely something metal." I ease forward a little further. Suddenly there's a bright white light around me and I shield my eyes.

"What's going on?" Ava yells.

"I don't know!" I yell back. I wait a second or two but nothing else happens. I move my hands away from my face and my eyes slowly adjust to the light, which appears to be coming from the roof of the caves. I walk over to Ava and put my hand on her shoulder. "It's ok, it was just the lights," I say, but something feels off. Why are there lights?

Ava stands up straight and looks around the room with me. "I don't understand."

We're certainly not in the caves we stepped into before. No, now we're standing in a polished metal tube with sleek bright lights hanging from the ceiling. It somehow feels familiar.

Then it hits me like a bag of bricks. "I've seen this before."

"Wait, really?"

"Yeah, on the first day of school I got super lost—"

"Totally not like you," she jokes.

"I'm serious," I say.

"Sorry, go on."

"I was walking around the tunnels of the school and found one just like this. Same metal flooring and everything."

"That's a weird coincidence, but we're not too far from the school. Maybe they're a part of it," she says.

As we walk down the tunnel together, another thought pops into my mind.

"The library," I say, stopping in my tracks.

"The library?" Ava stops next to me.

"The bookshelves are in the same kind of tunnels," I say, remembering back to the hallway with the old android manuals. Those had the same metal floors, just like this one.

"But that's nowhere near here," Ava says. I start walking again and she follows. "Why would they have the same tunnels?"

"I don't know. But there's something going on with them."

The tunnel comes to a sharp turn and we turn along it into another long stretch. A little ways ahead of us the lights are out. Ava and I walk towards the dark section, stopping just ahead of it.

I turn towards her. "Together?"

"Together." She reaches over and grabs my hand tightly.

We step into the dark area and, just like before, another bright light turns on. We're not standing in a hallway, but rather a large circular room with giant white columns stretching up to the ceiling. My jaw drops. The ceiling is covered in large murals of the night sky with thousands of tiny painted stars looking down on us. Must've taken forever to paint all that.

"What is this place?" Ava asks. Neither of us lets go of each other's hand.

"I have no idea." I walk further into the room. My eyes are drawn upwards to a large dark globe with giant brass rings floating around it, suspended above a circular table decked out with a variety of computer screens. Neither the globe nor the rings move, despite not seeming to be attached to any-thing. It's like they're just frozen in midair.

"Come look at this." Ava pulls me to-wards something on the floor.

"It's an android." I look at his face, the same familiar face from all around town. He's propped up against one of the columns, com-pletely inactive, and his chest panel is left hanging wide open. "The power cell has been removed from this one too," I say. Ava looks concerned.

WARDENCLYFFE

"What do you think did that?" I feel her grip get tighter around my hand.

"I think it was the woman in the red coat." I look around the rest of the room. "Let's see if she left anything else here."

Ava and I turn around to explore the rest of the room and see a large metal sign on the opposite wall. The sign says 'Wardenclyffe'.

Ava notices it at the same time as me. "I thought Wardenclyffe was the lighthouse."

"It is." I examine the sign closely. The lettering looks exactly the same as the one from the lighthouse.

"Then why's it here too?" She looks over at me and our eyes meet again. I'm suddenly aware of how long I've been holding her hand and awkwardly loosen my grip. I twirl my hair, trying to play it off.

"No idea." I walk over to where the sign is hanging over a massive door. The whole door is covered in everything from dents and scratches to what looks like a series of scorch marks. There's a small panel next to it that has been ripped open, leaving a mess of wires dangling from it. "This must be what she was trying to get into."

"I wonder why," Ava says. We scour the rest of the room, looking for any other clues as to what it might be for, but come up empty.

"It doesn't look like there's too much else here," I say. My stomach growls loudly.

"What was that?" Ava asks.

"I think I'm a little hungry," I say sheepishly. She laughs loudly and it echoes through the room. My face turns red. "Come on, we've been in here a while and I had a small lunch," I say.

"Well, how about we call it a day and head back?"

"Sounds good." I pause, thinking about her hand in mine. "Hey, Ava?"

She turns back to me. "Yeah? What's up?"

"Would you like to go get dinner with me?" I can hear my voice shaking a little bit.

"You mean like—"

"Like a date." I lay it out there and she smiles.

"I'd love that very much." She walks back over, grabs my hand, and we walk back out of the tunnel towards the cave entrance again, the lights turning off behind us as we leave. It's easy to push down any lingering thoughts I had about the caves and the woman in the red coat for the time being. Despite the cold breeze and freezing temperature, her hand feels warm in mine.

The sun has gotten much lower in the sky by the time we walk back around the edge of the rocks towards June. We pass the lighthouse, my eyes and thoughts lingering briefly on the Wardenclyffe sign above the door. As we reach the town there are a bunch of people out and about on the streets. I let go of Ava's hand.

"I wanna stop at my place first," I tell her. "Want to meet me at the market near the flower shop?"

"We going to eat at the flower shop?" she jokes.

"No, I just thought it would be a good place to meet before we go out to eat," I explain.

"So where are you taking me?"

"It's a surprise," I say.

She smiles. "Fine, I'll meet you back near the flower shop in, like, an hour, ok?"

"Sounds perfect," I give her a big hug and we head off in opposite directions. I walk quickly back up to my house. Inside, my mom is sitting in front of the fireplace with a large notebook and pencil.

"Hey, Olive, how was school?" She closes the notebook and puts the pencil behind her ear.

"It was good, we gave our presentation on the edelweiss today." I walk over and give her a hug. "What about you?"

"My editor wants a chapter of the new book. I'm supposed to post it to her soon," she says.

"Is it done yet?" I look at the notebook in her hand.

"Not quite, just hasn't really clicked yet. I'm sure it will soon, though." She places the notebook on the table in front of her. "You sticking around for dinner tonight?"

I shake my head. "Nah, I'm gonna head out for dinner. Just wanted to come change first."

"Oh yeah, any place I know?"

"Yeah, you remember that noodle shop we found together last week? I'm going there again," I say.

"Oh yeah? By yourself?" Her voice raises like she knows I'm hiding something.

"No…"

"Who're you going with? Anyone I know?" she pries.

"Yes, I'm going with Ava," I say, and run over towards the stairs. "And if I don't get ready soon I'm going to be totally late."

Within seconds, I'm up in my room pulling stuff out of my closet. As I'm rifling through the clothes, a small scrap of blue paper falls out of the pocket of something. I reach down and gently pick it up. Oh yeah, I'd totally forgotten about this. I slowly unfold it, careful not to damage the old blue paper. It feels just as delicate as the book it fell out of. I lay it out on it on the desk, my eyes wandering over the illustrations. Before long, my mind drifts back to Ava and our date, so I go back to picking out clothes. I'll look at it later.

I finally find the outfit I was looking for, brown corduroy pants and a nice maroon sweater that I found in one of the shops up here. This is one of my favorite outfits, right up there with the one I wore for the first day of school. I change in record time and run back downstairs.

"See you later." Mom gives me a knowing smile as I pull on my coat and run out the door.

"See ya!" I say, already halfway out the door as I say this. I fly down the streets until I reach the flower shop, where Ava stands waiting for me. She's wearing a beautiful new coat with little flowers embroidered along the bottom. Her hair, which she usually wears pulled back, hangs down over her shoulders. She looks amazing.

I run up to her. "You wait long?"

"Nah, just got here a little while ago," she says. Punctual as always.

"Ok, let's go." I grab her hand and we walk towards the market district.

"You gonna tell me where we're going?" she asks as we walk down the steps.

"It's still a surprise." I lead the way until we arrive at the restaurant. I recognize it by the bowl of noodles carved into the wood above the doorframe. I pull open the thick wooden door for Ava and she steps inside.

The interior is just how I remember it, wooden lanterns hanging down from the ceilings with dim warm light coming from them and small wooden tables and chairs that match the rest of the decor. We're greeted by a man standing at a little podium by the entrance.

"Hey, Ava," he says.

"Hey, Rico."

"Let me grab you two a spot." He leads us towards one of the tables.

"You've been here before?" I ask Ava, feeling a little embarrassed that she's already been here.

"Of course, silly. You forget I've lived here sixteen years." She takes off her coat, revealing a deep blue dress underneath. I also catch a glint of her silver necklace as she hangs her coat over the back of the chair next to her. I take off my coat too and sit across from her.

"Well, I hope you still enjoy," I say nervously.

"Oh, I love this place," she says. "You picked well." She winks at me and my heart flutters with nerves and joy.

"I like your necklace," I say.

"Thanks, it was a gift from my mom." She holds up the silver chain and the blue crystal pendant catches the light from the hanging lantern above us. "You look cute tonight."

"So do you," I say nervously. Rico comes back over to the table with two large bowls of noodles and places one in front of each of us.

"Here you two go. I'll be right back with the rest."

"Smells really good," Ava says.

Rico returns once more with a large platter and places a bunch of bowls onto the table, some with meat, others with herbs and spices.

"Enjoy," he says, before heading back to the front of the restaurant. Ava and I begin adding things to our bowls of noodles. I start with the broth, then take a handful of the herbs and sprinkle them over. I grab the chopsticks from the table and mix everything together. To finish it off, I place some of the meat on top of the noodles.

I watch Ava as she builds her bowl too. I can tell from watching her that she's done this before, she manages to effortlessly combine all the things into the bowl quickly and smoothly. The way she finishes it looks so professional. Mine doesn't look quite as neat as hers but it still smells incredible.

"So why do you like exploring so much?" Ava asks as we dig into our food.

"I've always done it, since I was a kid. Back in University there were so many places to see. And my dad encouraged it a lot. He always traveled for his research so he thought I should too. I guess I grew to like it a lot," I say.

"Do you want to be a scientist like him?"

"Well, I'm sure he'd like that a lot, but I'm not really sure. Like, what he does is interesting but I kind of want to do my own thing, you know?"

"What would you want to do?"

"I always thought it would be cool to be a historian. Or like an archeologist," I admit.

"Really? Why those?"

"I'm just fascinated by all the old stuff out there. Even here in June there's stuff that's been here for ages, like Wardenclyffe. Plus, even if I don't become a scientist, I do really like the travel part."

"Yeah, I guess there would be a lot of travel for stuff like that. And there's a lot we don't know about all that old stuff," she says.

"Exactly. Like, the pre-flooding history is pretty limited. On the way up to June, we drove by this massive old structure in the ice, and I asked but no one has any idea what it is. It could be anything," I explain. "Even back in University there were rumors of entire cities that are underwater now. Can you imagine what those must be like? The kinds of

things that are lost under the ocean?" I realize
I've been talking for a while. Ava has her
head rested on one of her hands. "Sorry I'm
talking so much."

"I don't mind. You're so passionate about
everything, it's one of the reasons I like you
so much," she responds, and I feel my face go
completely red.

"What about you?" I ask her, swirling the
noodles in my bowl around with a chopstick.

"I'm not really sure yet." She looks pen-
sive. "I like playing music."

"I didn't know you played! What kind?" I
ask.

"Well, I've been playing the flute for a
couple of years," she says,

"You'll have to play for me sometime."

"I promise I will." We each pause and eat
some more food, before Ava continues, "I
always thought it would be cool to play in
one of the big cities someday."

"Like in one of the performance halls?"

"Is that where they do music shows?" she
asks.

I realize she's probably never seen one in
person. "Yeah! I'll tell you all about it sometime. Maybe someday we can even go visit
one together," I joke.

"I would really love that," she says.

As we finish our food, I tell her stories
about growing up in University, and in return

she tells me about her life in June. By the time Rico comes over to take our plates away, I've completely lost track of how much time has passed and I realize we're some of the only ones left in the restaurant.

Not wanting to be rude, we both grab our coats and walk out. The streets are now only illuminated by the old streetlights, the sun long since set.

"This was wonderful," Ava says.

"It really was," I agree.

We stand and stare at each other, neither of us saying a word. I can feel my heart beating out of my chest. I lean in for a hug and suddenly I feel her lips on mine. The kiss is quick, but the delicate smell of her floral perfume lingers as she pulls away with a big smile.

"See you at school tomorrow." She blushes and lets go of my hand before awkwardly waving and running off in the direction of her house.

I stand there completely lovestruck as I reach up and touch my lips; I can still feel hers there. The entire walk home, I'm just floating on a cloud.

CHAPTER SIX

THE HATCH

It's still early when I'm woken up by a bright sunbeam in my face. I roll over to the other side of my bed where the sunbeam can't quite reach. The only thought in my mind is of going to school and seeing Ava. It's been a couple of days since our date and even though I've seen her since, I still can't stop thinking about it. With her as my motivation, I finally pull myself out of bed.

As I'm standing up, my eyes catch a glimpse of the folded-up piece of paper on my desk. I haven't really given it much thought since the other night. The deep-blue paper is covered in a mess of delicate white lines like a blueprint, but almost every line is so faded it's hard to determine what its purpose is. I've been trying to make some sense of it for days. I thought maybe it was related to the lighthouse, since that's where I found it, but none of the lines I can make out seem to match up with anything, so I quickly scrapped that theory.

I rotate the paper and that's when I notice something familiar. Among some of the faded sections, I can just barely make out a small circle with what looks like a drawing of a globe inside, surrounded by rings. It's super faded, so I'm not entirely sure what I'm seeing, but could that be the same room Ava and I were exploring the other day? I run my fingers along one of the lines coming off of it.

Then would that make these other lines the tunnels out to the caves? I trace the line back out towards the edge of the paper, and as I look at the rest of it, the pieces finally start to click together. It's not blueprints at all, it's a map. There's another long line coming up from that same spot with the globe illustration. That must be the door we couldn't get through with all the dents and scorch marks. And that line continues up the page, branching into hundreds of other slightly faded lines. It's hard to make out the full details but these can't all be tunnels, right? That would make whatever this is absolutely massive.

As I'm scouring over the details of the page, I manage to make out a couple of letters towards the top that read 'ENTER'. Wait, so if this is a map maybe I can figure out where these markings line up. I grab the paper and run over to the map of June on my wall. I hold them up next to each other, trying to map where everything would line up. I manage to line up the picture of the globe with where the caves are, but something feels off. If this is right, then that would mean all these lines run directly under June. And if these lines are tunnels, does that really mean there are tunnels running under the entire city? And if so, what could they possibly be for?

I look at the 'ENTER' label on the map again. If I'm estimating right, it looks like it could be up north of the city in the tundra. It's hard to be sure but I don't think it'd be too far out there. I look over at the clock in my room. I can at least take a quick look before school starts. I quickly get dressed, tuck the map into my pants, and run downstairs.

"You want some food?" Dad asks.

"I'm just gonna grab something to go." I run over to the kitchen and grab a small pastry from the breadbox.

"Where you off to this early?"

I tuck the pastry into my coat pocket. "Just wanted to go do some exploring."

"Stay safe," he says.

I run over and give him a hug before running out the door. I've been putting off telling him about the woman in the red coat or any of the tunnels we've found yet, mostly because I'm worried he'll make us stop checking them out.

I hurry up the steps towards the top street level, stopping underneath the wooden sign, totally unchanged from the last time I was here. I pull the map out of my pocket, fighting to keep the delicate paper shielded from the wind. I look at where one of the lines ends right next to the 'ENTER' label. It looks like it's a little northwest. I hold the paper in front of the landscape before me, like it should somehow make it easier to understand. But I'm determined to find it.

I walk forward into the tundra, the icy ground crunching loudly beneath my feet. Small twiggy plants poke up through the flat landscape, mostly barren but a couple still with brown leaves hanging on. With not a hill in sight, the wind bites at my face as I trudge further away from June.

My foot catches on something and I barely stop myself from falling. Jutting out of the ground is a weird orange crystal. It catches the sunlight, casting orange refractions over the nearby snow. I use my foot to dust away the snow and find more of the same crystal embedded into the surrounding rock.

I give the biggest crystal a kick with my boot but it doesn't budge at all. Looking closely, there seem to be dark black veins running through it. I quickly pull out the holo-recorder, record for a couple of seconds, then keep walking north.

I walk for about twenty minutes, scanning the landscape for any sign of the entrance. As I'm considering turning back, I notice a small, raised spot ahead of me. I quickly run over to it and find what looks like a large metal door in the ground. I dust off the snow, looking for some kind of handle to open it, but instead find a small plaque, completely covered in a layer of ice, which reads, 'DO NOT ENTER. WARDENCLYFFE FACILITY SEALED JULY 11 2308'.

"Wardenclyffe Facility?" I say out loud. The words feel weird in my mouth. What does that mean? If the lighthouse isn't Wardenclyffe then what is?

But the real thing gnawing at my brain is the date. I run my fingers over the ice-covered plaque. 2308. That was hundreds of years ago, even before the flooding. Has this really been sealed-up for that long?

My brain races thinking about what might be down there. But my thoughts grind to a halt as soon as I hear a distant chiming coming from the direction of the town. Oh crap, I have to get to class.

I take one last look at the hatch in the ground. I'm totally going to come back here later with Ava. Racing back towards town, my feet sink into the snow with each step, crunching loudly. I reach the edge of June and run under the wooden sign, flying down the

steps towards the lowest street. This might be the first time I've actually run straight down all the flights of stairs in the city at once, at least without stopping somewhere along the way. By the time I'm about halfway down, I get into a good rhythm.

There are still a bunch of people walking around, getting ready to start their day. Although strangely it seems like fewer people have their androids in tow. In fact, it's mostly just been other people out today. But it's hard to pay any of them too much mind when all I can think about is telling Ava about what I found.

I reach the bottom street level and run towards the school. Admittedly, running along this street while I'm late to school has become something of a regular habit. But unlike the other days, I'm not going to let myself get distracted by things like ice skating or the woman in the red coat. And, as if the thought itself had summoned her, I notice her walking out towards the docks. I weigh the choice of following her or going to school, but ultimately school wins out. I'll just have to catch up with her another time. After all, I'd much rather see Ava than chase after the woman in the red coat again.

We're back to having art class first, so I make my way through the tunnels to the art building. When I catch a glimpse of Ava walking ahead of me, I pull out my holo-recorder, turn it on, and run up beside her.

"Hello, my darling!" I say, surprising her.

She jumps, then turns to me and notices the holo-recorder. "What's it today?"

"We're going on an adventure today!"

Ava rolls her eyes sarcastically. "Oh, are we really?"

"Yes! I've found a secret hatch north of the town!" I exclaim, drawing attention from a bunch of the other kids walking nearby.

"And what, we're just going to go explore it?" Ava asks.

"Of course. I didn't even tell you the best part yet!"

"Oh, and what's that?"

"It's apparently from before the flooding!" I say.

Ava stops smiling. "What do you mean?"

"I found the entrance buried in the snow, but apparently it was all abandoned before the flooding happened."

"Wait, but how would you know that?"

"There was a seal from when it was closed. The date was hundreds of years ago."

"There's no way a place like that is safe," Ava says.

"Oh, come on, if it was safe where would the fun be?"

"And did you tell your dad about it?" Ava asks.

I pause. "Not yet…"

"You always find the most creative ways to get us into trouble," she says, but I notice a small smile on her face.

"You know you love it," I say.

"Well, give me that." Ava reaches over and grabs the holo-recorder out of my hands. "If you're going to make us do this, I want it on record that it was your idea, ok?"

"Fine," I say into the holo-recorder, "my name is Olivia, and tomorrow this chicken and I are going to explore someplace super cool."

"Wait, hold on." Ava holds up her hand to me and we both stop walking.

"What's up?"

"It's not in focus, give me a sec." She taps the holo-recorder a couple of times before pointing it back towards me.

"You good?" She gives me a thumbs up. I smile and continue, "My name is Olivia and tomorrow the two of us are going to explore a cool hatch I found."

"How'd you even find it?" Ava asks as we reach the classroom.

"Oh, wait, let me show you, I found an old map," I say. Ava lowers the holo-recorder as we walk over to our seats. I pull out the map from my pocket and hand it to her. She passes back the holo-recorder and I hit the stop button.

She looks over the map. "Is it today or tomorrow?"

"What are you talking about?"

"When you first came over you said we were going on an adventure today. But then you said tomorrow," she says, looking up from the map. "Which is it?"

"Oh, yes, I changed my mind. I think we need more time to fully explore everything. We should save it for the weekend."

"Ah." She goes back to looking at the map.

Tim walks into our classroom, wearing the same paint-covered apron as always, but today he's added a thick knit cap to the ensemble. It suits him. "Who wants to be our drawing model this morning?" he asks the class. My hand shoots up. "Olivia, love the enthusiasm. Everyone set up your easels."

I don't have the heart to tell him I just want to model since I really suck at drawing. The class flips their papers to a blank page as I walk over to the table with all the random props and clothing. I pick up a fancy-looking coat, long and black with glittering gold lace. I also grab a small flat hat and pull it onto my head. Then under the pile I notice an old sword. Oh, I absolutely have to pick that up.

I walk over to the pedestal and strike a fun pose, holding the sword over my head. The metal is heavy.

"Ok, everyone, we'll take five minutes on this pose before switching it up," Tim says.

I hear all the kids in the class start sketching on their easels. I'm facing away from Ava, but I can still feel her looking at me and hear her charcoal moving against the paper.

I hold the pose as still as I possibly can, but the weight of the sword is definitely getting to me. My arm is sore and starting to shake.

"Ok, let's switch up the pose," Tim finally says, and I drop my arm in relief. This time I turn around to face Ava and point the sword in her direction, switching it to my other hand, which is much less tired. I smile at her and she gives me a big smile back, then starts sketching again, looking up at me every couple of seconds. I feel like she's only staring at my face, not that I mind at all. I could stare at her like this for the whole class if I had to.

"Ok, everyone, let's wrap-up our warm-up for today," Tim says. I don't know why but this pose felt like I was doing it for a much shorter time. I walk back over to the table, take off the coat and hat, and drop them onto the pile, along with the sword. Then I walk back over to my seat and sit down next to Ava. I look at her easel and see her illustration of me.

"That's amazing," I say.

"You really think so?"

"Yeah, you made me look so much cooler than I actually am," I joke.

Tim gets up in front of the class and starts lecturing about art history again, but we carry on our conversation, quiet enough not to be heard by the others.

"Well, I think you're pretty cool," she whispers, and I blush a little bit.

"I think you're cool too," I tell her. "So did you get a chance to look at it?" I point at the map in front of her.

"Are these really all part of the same thing?" She runs her fingers all over the lines.

"I think so. And do you see this here?" I point to the spot that says 'ENTER'. "That has to be the door I found this morning."

"Why do you think that?"

"Well, there really wasn't much else up that way. I feel like if there was something else, I would've come across it," I explain. Then I notice Tim has stopped lecturing and is staring at the two of us.

"Sorry," Ava says.

We stop talking and Tim returns to his lecture. "As I was saying, next week will be our final class discussing the Return-To-Nature artistic movement before moving on to our next module."

I whisper to Ava, "Come over to the lighthouse after school so we can plan for tomorrow."

She nods as Tim discusses various types of old pigments.

After art class wraps up, Ava and I walk to our science class together. We arrive at the classroom along with a bunch of other kids. As we take our seats, I notice the edelweiss flower from our presentation hanging above the corner of the blackboard, tied up with a little string and held there by a small thumbtack. Mrs. Barlowe arrives and places her bag softly onto her desk.

"Welcome, class. As I mentioned yesterday, we will be discussing AI in today's class," she starts. "Does anyone remember what AI stands for?" A couple of hands raise. She points to one of the boys.

"It's Artificial Intelligence, right?" he asks.

"That's correct." She writes 'ARTIFICIAL INTELLIGENCE' on the board behind her. "Anyone want to guess what it was used for?" Fewer hands raise this time.

She calls on one of the girls. "Yes, Barb?"

"Was it for computers?" Barb says timidly.

"Among other things," Mrs. Barlowe starts. "We believe that AI was first introduced sometime in the early 2300s. It began as a navigational system but quickly became used for things like vending machines, early-model androids, and even terraforming," she explains. "And the biggest feature was that the AI systems were designed to learn and grow on their own."

Someone near us raises their hand and Mrs. Barlowe points to her.

"Are there any things that still use AI?" the girl asks.

"I'm afraid not." Mrs. Barlowe shakes her head. "Most of that old tech was never maintained. I doubt there's a single piece of machinery left that still has AI running in it."

She continues to talk about AI for the rest of the class, but I feel my mind drifting. With the sun coming in through the window and heating up the room a little, I can feel myself beginning to doze off. I'm still stuck thinking about those tunnels, wondering how they're all connected. And, more importantly, what they're for.

"You coming?" Ava asks. I snap back to reality and she's standing in front of me as all the other kids filter out of the room.

"Class is over?" I ask, and she laughs.

"Of course. You were pretty zoned out, huh?"

I grab my bag and get up quickly. "Yeah, hard to stay focused," I say. We leave the classroom together and walk towards our next classes. We stop at a split in the tunnels.

"Well, I'm off this way," she says, giving me a hug. "We can head over to the lighthouse after school."

I walk to my next class alone, thinking about how the afternoon classes would drag on without her to keep me company. And sure enough, the afternoon drags on forever. I listen to lectures about big ships that went into space from my astronomy professor and learn about old music from before the flooding from my music professor. She plays old music on a machine that sounds rough and full of static. The music bounces around the room but it feels weird to be listening to it recorded instead of played by an actual person. It hardly seems to compare to the shows back in University.

Finally, the bell rings and classes wrap up for the day. I rush back to meet Ava at the entrance, where she tells me about her classes as we walk to the lighthouse.

"So, what do we need to bring for tomorrow?" she asks.

"I'm not really sure." I realize I don't know what we're going to be in for on our trip.

"Well, I'm sure we'll figure it out," Ava assures me. As we're walking along the path to the lighthouse, I see the woman in the red coat walking towards us. As she gets closer, she notices us.

"Oh, hello there," she says.

I feel myself sweating a little bit. "Hey," I say.

She looks at me closely. Her eyes are deep brown and piercing. "I remember you. We met on the bus into June."

"Yeah, that was my first day here," I say. "I'm Olivia."

"I'm Ava," Ava says, jumping into the conversation.

"Ava and Olivia. Good names. Nice to meet the two of you." The woman reaches out her hand and shakes both of ours. She wears thick leather gloves that match the red of her coat. "My name is Saffron."

"What're you doing up here, Saffron?" I ask.

"Just taking a stroll around the city," she says. Somehow, I don't believe her. But I'm also trying not to let on that I've basically been stalking her. "What about you two?"

"We're hanging out in the lighthouse," I say.

"Oh yes, Wardenclyffe." She turns around to look at the lighthouse. "You two have fun." She turns back, gives us a big smile, and continues past us. Ava and I watch her walk away, and the second she's out of earshot I turn to Ava.

"She's definitely up to something, right?" I ask.

"Oh yeah," Ava agrees. "Something about her just feels off."

We walk up to the lighthouse and head inside together.

"Do you think she was here?" I ask.

"Do you think who was here?" my dad says, catching the tail end of our conversation.

"Dad, have you seen a woman in a big red coat recently?" I ask, and he nods.

"You mean Saffron? Of course, she was just here. She asked to look for something in the bookshelves upstairs," he says.

"And you let her?"

"Why wouldn't I?" He looks confused. "She was one of Kai's lab assistants," he explains as he tinkers with a piece of machinery on his desk.

"Wait, really?" I ask.

He holds up a hand and presses record on a small holo-recorder. That one must be his. It looks like a slightly different model than mine.

"Journal Entry 33486-PD. Today I'm testing Power Drive 215. Here goes." He flips a switch on the large machine in front of him on the desk and it loudly hums to life. The room pulses with vibrations and the lights around us dim. The desk shakes violently under the weird-looking machine until there's a sudden spark and flash of light. The vibrations abruptly stop. The burned-out machine sits there in silence, doing nothing but emitting a small plume of smoke from one of its panels. Dad grabs some folders from another desk and fans the smoke away.

"So, about that woman," I say, trying to distract him from the less-than-successful test he just ran.

"Yeah, don't know much about her beyond the fact that she worked here," he says, still distracted. He flips his holo-recorder off and starts taking apart the large machine. As he pulls off the first panel, I catch a glimpse of the melted wires inside. Doesn't really look like there's too much to salvage but I decide to keep that thought to myself.

I pull Ava towards the staircase. "We're gonna head upstairs and study."

"Let me know if you two need anything," he says as we climb up the staircase.

I walk out onto the second floor and look around the bookcases. That's when I notice a book sitting on the nearby desk that wasn't there earlier.

"What do you think she was looking for?" Ava asks. I pick up the book, recognizing it instantly. *A Midsummer Night's Dream.*

"I know exactly what she was looking for." I pull out the folded map from my pocket.

"Why do you think that's what she was looking for?" Ava asks.

"Because I found it here," I say, holding up the copy of *A Midsummer Night's Dream* in my other hand.

"Wait, really?" She grabs the map from me and quickly unfolds it. "Do you think she was looking for a way into the tunnels?" Ava examines the paper closely, flipping it over and looking at the back side.

"She has to be, right? I mean, when we found that room with the globe it looked like someone was trying to open up the door there. And that was on the map too." I point at the faded illustration of the globe with the rings around it.

"Maybe she hasn't been able to find a way in yet," Ava says.

We sit down at one of the small tables across the room.

"But that still doesn't explain what she was doing down there. Or why I caught her taking the power cells out of the androids in that old building either," I say.

"Yeah, that doesn't make any sense." Ava puts the paper onto the table in front of us. "Are you sure we should be trying to explore this place?"

"Of course I am! Why wouldn't we?" She seemed so on board before.

"What if it's dangerous? Like, that woman could be trouble. And maybe it's all closed up for a reason," she argues.

"I'm sure it's not bad!"

"What about that plaque you mentioned near the door about when it was sealed? You said that was from before the flooding. Who knows what we're gonna find down there," she says.

"Yeah, but that's the exciting part! Like, imagine the history we could find down there," I say.

She smiles at me. "You probably would make a good archeologist." I sense her relaxing a little bit more. "Tell me what we need for the trip," she says.

I think it over for a couple of seconds. "Well, we should probably bring some light along. I think we have a lantern back in our house. I can grab that for us."

"Yeah, that's probably a good thing to have."

I walk over to the other wall and pick up one of the crowbars that my dad and I had been using to pull off the wood paneling from all the walls.

"This might help too," I say, holding it up.

"I hope we don't need that." She laughs. "You know what else we should probably grab too?"

"What?" I have no idea what she's thinking of.

"We should bring some food along."

"Oh, like a picnic!" Although June doesn't seem like it has too many good areas for picnicking, apart from where we found the edelweiss flower. I imagine us sitting in one of the tunnels together on a small picnic blanket, but it doesn't feel particularly romantic.

"I was thinking in case we end up out exploring for a while."

She makes a good point. Who knows how long we could be down there.

"Oh, that's true. How about we start gathering stuff up and packing tonight and then we can meet at the northern sign tomorrow morning?" I suggest.

"Sounds like a plan to me."

I lean over the table and give her a kiss. Then she runs back down the stairs and I start looking around the lighthouse for other things that might be helpful on our trip, starting with one of the other crowbars in the room. For Ava.

The next morning, I wake up bubbling with excitement. I finish packing up my bag, grabbing the lantern I stashed in my closet last night. I found it hidden at the back of one of our kitchen cupboards, so I doubt it'll be missed anytime soon.

I also pull out a small piece of string and tie it in a loop around the end of the holo-recorder. I pull the string tight to make sure it's secured, then put it on over my head where it hangs neatly like a necklace. I honestly can't believe I didn't think of this earlier.

I tuck the crowbars into the bag, along with some extra rags so they don't clang together. I pull a pair of thick denim pants out of the closet, perfect for exploring, and a long sleeve shirt to go with them. It's made from a thick, warm fabric that always makes me feel super cozy.

I also grab my dad's hand-me-down coat. The leather is old and worn but the inside is lined with thick fur. It's probably the warmest thing I own, perfect for exploring the cold tundra, even if it is a little big on me. I quickly change, pull the bag over my shoulder and run downstairs.

"You're up early," Mom says from the table in the living room.

"Hey, Olive," Dad says from the kitchen. He's busy prepping some delicious-smelling breakfast food.

"What're you making?" I ask him.

"We got some eggs from the neighbors. I'm making omelettes," he says. "You gonna join us?" he asks, adding some chopped scallions into the pan.

"I was gonna go meet Ava. Mind if I take her one?" I ask, giving my biggest puppy-dog-eyes. He laughs.

"Yeah, sure, just give me a few minutes." He keeps cooking, moving the pan over the small flame of the oven. I sit down at the table with my mom.

"What're you two up to today?" she asks.

"We were just going to explore the city," I say.

"If you're looking for a cool spot, your dad and I just discovered this wonderful little gallery space," she says.

"Oh yeah, it's right down near the ice shelf," Dad adds from the kitchen.

"They've got some wonderful pieces in there. Seems like the trade though the city also brings in some pretty amazing artwork," Mom continues.

"That does sound pretty cool. I'll have to check that out." Maybe that can be a nice date for Ava and I tomorrow. My dad comes over and hands me two omelettes wrapped in a small cloth and tied with twine. I can feel the heat coming off them as I tuck them into my backpack.

"Tell Ava we say hi," Mom says, as I give her and Dad a big hug.

"I will, love you both lots." I wave good-bye as I leave the house, quickly running up the steps to the top of the city. When I reach the gate, I see Ava waiting there wearing an outfit I've never seen her in before. Usually she's in a long dress but today she's got on a pair of pants almost like mine and a thick wool coat with a dark plaid pattern. I run up and give her a kiss on the cheek.

"You wait long?" I ask her.

"Just a few minutes," she says.

"Well, I brought some food for us so maybe once we get up there we can eat it together," I say.

"Sounds nice."

We walk under the gate together onto the frozen tundra. Unlike yesterday, there's a harsh breeze blowing across the landscape making it a lot harder to see. We stay close to each other as the wind kicks up a flurry of snow.

"It's this way," I say, leading us in the direction I remember from the day before.

Ava grabs onto my arm and pulls me close. "So how far away is it?"

"I think I was walking for a little over twenty minutes last time." We walk against the wind and it makes for slow progress. "Might take a little longer this time," I joke.

"Well, we've got the whole day, right?"

"Of course."

She stumbles a little but catches herself on my arm.

"What're those?" At her feet are a bunch of orange crystals.

"Oh yeah, I saw those before. Must mean we're going in the right direction," I assure her.

"But, like, what are they?"

"Some weird crystal, I guess. Why?"

"Aren't those the same rocks that're in the lighthouse?" She kicks at one of them. I remember all of Kai's rocks in the lab back at Wardenclyffe and realize she's probably right.

"Oh yeah, I guess those were the same ones Kai had," I say.

"They're kind of pretty," she says.

"Maybe I can make you a necklace out of one," I joke. We keep walking past the crystal structures and after another few minutes I see something dark on the ground ahead of us. "I think that's it." I point to it and we walk over.

"Looks like you were right," Ava says as we arrive at the hatch. I lean down and brush some of the snow off, revealing a large circular wheel protruding from the middle of the door. I reach into the backpack and pull out the crowbars, holding one of them out to Ava.

"I really don't think they want this opened." She's examining the plaque next to the hatch.

"Let's try spinning the wheel," I say, try-ing to distract her with the crowbar.

She finally notices the crowbar in my hand. "Of course you brought these."

"Thought it might be useful," I say as she grabs the crowbar from me.

We wedge them into the metal spokes of the wheel and lean against them. As I put my whole weight against my crowbar, I feel the wheel start to spin. It gives off an unpleasant screech as metal grinds against metal

"It's actually working." The second Ava says this, the wheel jolts loose and we fall to the ground. The crowbars come loose too and fall onto the door.

"Look at that. Now we just have to get it open." I tug the wheel but the door doesn't budge. That's when I notice the edges of the door are caked with a thick layer of ice. I start chipping away at it with the crowbar and Ava joins in. After a few minutes, we've managed to clear the ice away and I tug on the wheel again.

"Here, let me try giving you some lever-age." Ava digs her crowbar under the edge of the door and pulls it back. I pull on the wheel a third time and it finally budges. The door's heavier than anything I've ever lifted but I keep pulling. As it inches open, Ava drops the crowbar and pushes from the other side.

I jump out of the way as the weight of the door shifts. It falls onto the snow with a muffled thud. Underneath is another metal door with a large lever on it that looks like a handle. Although luckily this one isn't covered in ice.

"Another door?" Ava asks. She sounds less enthusiastic than she had on the way up here, but in spite of that I still feel like the moment should be recorded. I tap the record button on the holo-recorder around my neck and it makes a quiet beep.

"So, care to tell us where we are, Ava?" I ask, still a little out of breath from lifting the door.

"We're somewhere where we're not supposed to be." Ava is still looking at the plaque from when the door was sealed.

"Oh, come on, I thought we had found your sense of adventure," I joke.

"Nope, you just dragged me along again." I turn the holo-recorder a little and point it at the second door.

"Well, let's go!" I say.

Ava reaches down to the door and pulls the large lever. The second door swings upwards and I step closer to it.

"It's open," Ava says. She looks inside the hole. "And it looks like there's a staircase."

I walk over next to her and look into the large, dark opening and see a small spiral staircase going down into the darkness.

"Well, ladies first," I say.

"You're a lady too!"

"Yeah, but I'm also holding the camera. You can't expect me to go down first!"

"That's such a cop-out," Ava says, looking at the camera around my neck. But she still smiles and steps onto the stairs. Now that we're here, I think she's warming up to it a little more. I step onto the staircase after her and we begin to climb down the stairs together.

CHAPTER SEVEN

THE INSTITUTE

There's a little bit of light on the stairs from the opening above us but as we climb deeper it becomes darker. The spiral staircase matches the one from the lighthouse except it's way narrower. Ava stops on a small landing and waits for me to catch up. The holo-recorder lets out a loud beep to inform us it's out of disc space. The beep echoes loudly around us.

"It's pretty dark," Ava says, looking around.

"I thought it might be." I unzip my bag and pull out the lantern. As I crank the handle, there's a loud whirring noise from the gears inside. After a few cranks, it glows brightly, illuminating the landing we're on but not much more than that. There's a small railing on the edge of the platform but all we see beyond that is darkness.

"Your turn." Ava pokes me towards the next set of stairs.

I laugh. She really has me there. "I guess that's fair," I say, leading the way down with the lantern, each of my steps echoing around us.

"Sounds like we're in a big room," she says.

"Yeah, probably why the light doesn't show us anything." I finally reach the bottom of the stairs with Ava right behind me. The light from the lantern shines across a flat metal floor which seems to be made from large, interconnected panels.

"What do you think this is?" Ava asks.

"It's hard to tell. Not really much around, is there?" I keep walking forward until suddenly a bright light turns on, nearly blinding me. My eyes adjust quickly and my jaw drops as I look around.

"Look at that," Ava says, looking around in shock.

This has to be the biggest room I've ever seen in my life. Giant panels stretch across the floor and up the towering walls where massive light fixtures hang, shining light into the room. You could easily stack three lighthouses on top of each other in here and still have room to spare. But the most unusual thing about the room is that it's completely empty, save for the spiral staircase we just walked down. Why would you build a room this big and not put anything inside it?

"I can't even imagine what this would be used for." I walk further in. On the other side of the room there are a series of large windows high up on the wall, but I can't see anything through them. It looks like there's a small door below them too.

"Hey, where's that map of yours?" Ava asks.

"Oh, right." I pull the map out of my pocket and unfold it.

Ava skims it over for a minute before she points at a large rectangle just below the 'ENTER' label. "We must be right here. And it looks like there's a lot more." She points to a whole series of rectangles next to the first one.

"I wonder what they are." I stare at the map then look up at the room again. I notice some words on the wall behind us, painted in towering red letters. "*Oceanus*," I read off the wall.

"What?"

I point up to the wall. "It's painted up there."

"What's that mean?"

"Beats me. I've never heard that word before," I say.

"Must have been important to paint it up there." She makes a good point. Each letter is at least ten feet high, definitely not something you'd do without reason.

"Let's try the door over there." We make our way over to the door and as we get closer I realize the windows are actually leaning outwards from the wall. By the time we're standing in front of the door, they're practically towering over us. I pull the handle and the door swings open effortlessly. We step through and, just like everywhere else, bright lights turn on to reveal a long metal hallway. There must be some kind of sensor.

Dozens of doors flank each side of the hallway, one every couple of feet, some tightly shut while others sit ajar. I poke my head into one of the open ones. Instantly, lights. The room's about the size of my bedroom. The only indication that there was ever something in here is the bundle of frayed wires coming out of the walls. Whatever they were attached to looks like it was ripped out.

I check a couple more rooms and they all seem to be in the same state. Some doors remain tightly shut but I don't try too hard to open them. We finally reach a small room at the end of the hallway with a few assorted tables, the first room we've found that actually has anything inside. Even if it is just a few boring-looking pieces of furniture.

"Wanna stop here for a little bit?" I ask.

"Sure. Probably good to pace ourselves." Ava laughs and we sit down at the table together. I open up my backpack and pull out the omelettes that my dad gave me. I pass one across the table to her and unwrap my own.

"This place is so weird," I say, biting into my omelette.

"Kind of creepy." She takes a couple bites from hers. "Wow, this is so good." She quickly finishes the rest of it.

"Yeah, my dad's a good cook," I say.

"What's the best thing he makes?"

"He used to make me a delicious carrot cake for my birthday." I think back to that cake. Always a little rough around the edges but the most delicious thing I've ever eaten.

"That sounds good. My family doesn't cook as much. I've been learning though." She folds up the cloth the omelette had been in and hands it back to me. I tuck it back into the bag.

"I bet you're a great cook," I flirt.

"I'm ok." She blushes, covering her face with her hands. She's absolutely adorable.

"You'll have to cook for me sometime," I say.

"You'd really want that?" she asks, lowering her hands.

"Of course! Maybe that can be our next date night." I reach across the table and hold her hands. Even though we're inside, it's still pretty cold in here and her hands are a little chilly. We sit here like this for another few minutes before she breaks the silence.

"You wanna keep exploring?"

I nod and we both get up from the table, still holding hands. There's a bunch of doors branching off of this room, so we pick one at random to explore next. We follow the hallway to its end where it empties onto a balcony and a room that leaves me speechless.

Stretching out below us is a massive circular room with brilliant white walls and smooth curved surfaces. The balcony we've emerged onto continues down along the outer wall of the room in a spiral, forming a ramp down to the lowest level, where it opens up into the massive space.

Towering in the center are two giant statues, just like the ones at the top of the lighthouse, except these ones are probably just as tall as the lighthouse itself and look like they've had most of the pieces broken off. Giant white chunks of stone lay around the base of each.

Ava holds my hand tightly. "What is this place?"

I think back to the plaque we saw before. "This must be the Wardenclyffe Institute," I say.

"Yeah, but what is that?"

"You've got me beat there," I admit.

She leans over the edge of the balcony. "It's massive."

I pull out the holo-recorder, quickly pop in a new disc, and start recording. Through the lens, I can make out a little more detail of the statues. It looks like they're standing on opposite ends of some kind of pond, and on closer inspection seem to have some kind of plants growing on them.

I turn off the holo-recorder. "I have to know what's down there," I say as I lead her down the ramp. I can't help myself from glancing down at the statues every couple of seconds, in awe of their sheer size.

The further down we go, the mustier the air gets. It smells damp, like a swamp, and I notice that the brilliant white stones that everything is constructed from are starting to look dimmer too. Patterned like someone spilled a drink over their surface and never bothered to clean it up.

Neither of us says anything for a bit, but eventually I try to start a new topic, just to fill the silence as we walk. "So my mom told me about this gallery space down by the ice shelf."

"Oh yeah, I think I've heard of that one. It's with all the art from the traders, right?" she asks.

"Yeah, I think that's what she said. Have you ever been?"

"Not yet," she says.

"We should go check it out sometime."

"You really think it's going to compare to this?" She gestures over the railing.

"Fair point. I don't think much will," I say. I suddenly notice a figure laying on the ramp ahead of us and rush over to find a man probably close to my dad's age. "It's a person." I feel for a pulse. Nothing. He's cold. I flip him onto his side and right where his left arm should have been is a mess of wires coming out of his shoulder socket.

"Why are there wires coming out of his shoulder?" Ava asks.

I look him over carefully. "He's an android," I say. Although I can hardly believe it myself.

"But he looks completely real. Like he's not just metal," Ava says.

He's wearing a nice-looking outfit, although despite its pristine condition it looks about a century or two out of date, like something you'd see in a history book. I unbutton the shirt and, sure enough, he's got the same chest panel as the other androids in June, despite his unique appearance. I open the panel to find a small power cell. It's totally inactive though. My guess is the glow faded from this one a long time ago.

"He must've been here since the place was sealed." I look at his face closely. "He looks completely different from the other ones in June."

"If his arm was still there, I never would've been able to tell," Ava says.

"Yeah, I doubt I would have either." I stand up from the android. "Let's keep going," I say. We continue down the ramp and I run my hands along the smooth white stones of the railing.

"There's another one." Ava points ahead to another figure on the ground. We walk up to this one and I inspect him. It's a different face, but definitely an android too.

"How many types of android are down here?" I ask.

"Beats me. There's only like five models up in June," Ava explains as we continue past him. The entire way down is littered with more of the old androids, every single one with a completely different face. Finally, we emerge onto the lowest level and into a massive courtyard of white stone. The bright lights shining from somewhere above makes it hard to look directly at the stone. Down at this level the air is so damp that every breath feels like I'm drinking water.

We walk further into the room, past the broken chunks of statue that lay scattered around us. A giant fist sits in a crater of cracked marble ahead of us, like it shattered the ground where it fell. Although the statues are broken, they're still awe-inspiring the way they tower over everything.

As we make our way towards the center of the room, the pond we saw from above comes into full view. Big stone steps lead up to the surface of the water and thick vines grow over the edge of the steps, flowing down them like water. I trudge through the vines until I reach the top step.

Thick moss grows up the feet of both statues. Next to the feet sits one of the heads, laying on its side and so overgrown with vines you can't make out its features anymore.

"Hey, come check this out," Ava calls over to me.

"What is it?"

She's back at the bottom of the stairs, tugging the vines off something. I run over and help her tug at the vines until we manage to uncover a metal sign. At the top are large letters that read 'WARDENCLYFFE INSTI-TUTE' with a map filling the space below.

"Wait a second." I pull out the map from my pocket and hold it up against the sign, using the flat surface to smooth out the wrin-kles in the paper.

"They're the same," Ava says as she ex-amines them both.

I run my fingers over the metal sign. "But look at this. It actually has labels." They're carved into the metal and, unfortunately, with

so many layers of rust and wear it's hard to make out what they all say.

"We should copy them onto our map," she says.

"Good idea," I grab a small pencil from my bag and quickly transcribe as many of the labels as possible. Some are easy to make out like 'ARCHIVE' and 'RESIDENTIAL', but others I can only decipher a couple of letters, like 'CO US' and just 'HER'. They feel incomplete but my mind can't fill in what words they could be. I write small but it's still tough to fit all the words onto the tiny map. I also try to fill in as many of the faded areas as I can.

Ava turns and looks around the room. "So where do you want to explore next?"

"Let's check out this section called 'Archive'." I point to it on the map. "Should be right near us."

I look around until I see an archway on the far wall. That must be it.

I lead us around the outer edge of the pond towards the other side. We pass by more giant chunks of the statue and I notice a mechanical arm sticking out from underneath one of them. My heart sinks a little, thinking of the android that was crushed under there. We pass by more of the androids on the way around the pond.

Ava looks at them sadly as we walk past. "What do you think happened to all of them?"

"I think their power cells must have run out," I say. Although that probably wasn't true for the one under the chunk of the statue back there.

"Why do you think that?"

"Well, I did some reading about them from one of the user manuals in the library. Apparently, their power cell is designed to last a hundred years before needing to be replaced," I explain.

"So you think they just ran out?"

"Well, yeah, the date up on that hatch of when this place was sealed was hundreds of years ago. Even if they were still running when it was sealed they wouldn't have lasted forever."

"It's pretty sad."

"Yeah, it really is. Maybe that's why Saffron was taking all of those power cells from the other androids. Do you think she was trying to reboot these ones?"

"That could be. But what makes these ones more important than the androids out in the city?"

"Not a clue. If we're lucky we might find some answers here."

We arrive at the large archway and step into what should be the archive, according to the map. The lights come up to reveal a long, kind of plain-looking room. Throughout are a series of stone pedestals, each with a different object sitting on top. It certainly looks like an archive.

We walk between the different pedestals, examining all the weird items on display. I stop in front of one with a white, slightly-translucent cube on it.

"I wonder what this is." I pick up the cube. I can barely even feel it in my hand. It's as light as air, neither hot nor cold. If not for being able to see it, I'd wonder if it was there at all.

"Are you sure it's ok to touch that?" Ava asks.

"Why wouldn't it be?" Right after I say this, there's a buzzing noise throughout the room.

"Please be reminded, the artifacts in the museum are not to be disturbed," a voice says. It sounds like it's coming from all around us.

I look around for the source of the voice, but there's no one about.

"What was that?" I ask.

"I think you should put it back," Ava says.

"Please return the artifact to its location. If you do not comply, you will be asked to leave," the voice continues.

"By who?" I say loudly into the room.

"Just put it back," Ava says.

I place the cube back onto the pedestal and the buzzing noise stops. The voice is also gone. I look closely at the pedestal and notice a small sign on it:

'COMA CUBE

This small cube was picked up on the exploratory mission of the Oceanus *spacecraft on its journey to the Coma Galaxy Cluster. It was identified as non-organic material. Origin unknown. It was classified with the remainder of the Coma artifacts in the collection.'*

"So it's a museum," I say, reading off the sign.

"Yeah, that's what the voice said," Ava says. "What's the Coma Galaxy Cluster?"

"I think I remember something about that in astronomy class but now I wish I had actually paid more attention." I was usually pretty zoned out during those lectures. I walk over to another pedestal, this one with a large piece of rock that's been split right down the middle. There's a small object embedded in each half of the stone, but I can't quite make out what it is. I clear the dust off this one's plaque and read the description:

'COMA FOSSIL

Recovered from rogue planetoid in the Coma Galaxy Cluster by the Oceanus *mission. Fossil carbon dating suggests approximate age of two billion years.'*

We walk deeper into the room. Every single pedestal has some kind of object on top of it. Most of them don't look like anything special, just random rocks and boring-looking objects. But just ahead of us, at the far end of the room, is a shadow of something big and orange. And as we get closer and more lights turn on, I realize what I'm seeing.

A massive orange crystal, just like the ones up on the tundra, is growing around the furthest pedestals. Some are still partly sticking out of the crystal, but most are embedded deep within.

"That's weird," I say.

"Well, isn't everything in this room?" she says.

"I mean, look at all those pedestals in there." I point inside the crystal structure.

"Oh yeah. There's a lot in there."

I look over the crystal. "Do you think it's growing?"

She looks confused. "Can a crystal grow?"

"I mean, it feels weird that they'd set up the room like this. And I'm pretty sure they can grow, depending on the conditions. This feels—" I stop talking.

"What is—" Ava starts, but I hold up my hand and she stops too. There's a weird scurrying sound coming from nearby.

I lean in super close to her. "Something's there," I whisper. She nods, and I creep slowly around the crystal structure, walking as softly as I possibly can, heading in the direction of the sound. I can see a faint blue glow shimmering though the crystal. It looks like it's moving. I peek my head around the corner and see a small blue lizard sitting on the ground.

The lizard is roughly the size of my palm and its whole body is glowing. It has jagged teeth, which I catch a glimpse of as it opens its jaw and bites into the orange crystal. Ava pokes her head around the corner too and sees the small lizard crunching on the crystal.

"What's that?" she asks.

The lizard stops eating and looks up at us with big, black eyes. I stay quiet for a few seconds. The lizard goes back to eating.

"It looks like a lizard, but not like any I've ever seen before," I say. I've never actually seen any kind of animal that glows like that. I reach my hand down to the lizard and it stops eating, looks at me carefully, then slowly approaches. When it's close enough, I gently brush the top of its head with the back of my hand. It closes its eyes, but as I place my hand down so I can sit, it catches on a sharp piece of crystal.

"Damn it," I shout.

"What happened?" Ava yells.

Our voices startle the lizard and chaos erupts. There's suddenly a flash of bright blue light and a loud bang as Ava and I are knocked backwards. I slowly pull myself up but the lizard is nowhere in sight.

"Are you ok?" Ava helps me up.

"I got cut on the crystal," I say. I look down at my palm and there's a shard of the orange crystal sticking out of my skin, blood dripping all over me.

"Here, stay still." Ava helps roll up the sleeve of my jacket, then shirt. I try to distract myself from the pain as she hurriedly digs around in her bag, eventually producing a small metal box.

"What's that?" I ask.

"First aid kit," she says with a little smile. "I had a feeling you might need it eventually." She opens up the box and pulls out a pair of tweezers from the assortment of medical supplies.

"I'm not that clumsy," I say.

She holds my hand down and carefully pulls the crystal shard out of my palm, then tosses it aside. Tears well up in my eyes from the pain.

"No, but you are a little reckless." She leans in and kisses my cheek. "And I worry." She pulls out a bottle and cloth, then pours some of the liquid from the bottle onto it. "This might sting a little." She holds it to the cut on my hand and I feel a sharp stinging.

"You said a little," I joke.

"Ok fine, I lied." She smiles as she cleans up the cut. Then she pulls out bandages and carefully wraps them around my hand, keeping pressure on my palm as she does.

"How did you learn how to do this?" I watch her as she works. She seems to be pretty skilled at this.

"My mom runs one of the small clinics in June," she says.

"Really? I had no idea." With my sleeve rolled up, I can feel a cool breeze coming through the room.

"Yup. I mean, you learned science stuff from your dad, right? Well, I learned first aid stuff from her. Mostly just the basics but still helpful." She finishes bandaging up my hand and starts packing the supplies back into the metal tin.

"Thanks," I say as she slips the first aid kit back into her bag and I roll my sleeve down. "Let's keep going." I'm eager to be anywhere the orange crystal isn't.

We continue past it and the rest of the podiums before passing through a large door at the back of the room. I nearly have a heart attack as the lights come up and there's a person sitting directly in front of us at a small desk. Ava and I scream but the person doesn't move.

"Is she an android?" Ava asks.

I walk over to get a closer look. She has deep wrinkles and grey hair that hangs down past her shoulders. She's also wearing a small pair of spectacles, through which I can clearly see the circuits on her eyes.

"Yes, she's definitely an android," I say. Usually they make them with really young faces but not with this one.

"Why's she look older than the others?" Ava asks, clearly thinking the same thing as me.

"I don't know. I'm still trying to figure out why all these androids have different faces."

There's a stack of books on the desk in front of the android and a small sign that reads 'CIRCULATION'.

"I think this is a library," I look around the rest of the room and my instinct is confirmed by rows and rows of bookshelves, stretching back further than I can see.

Every shelf is neatly lined with pristine books, each bound in dark leather covers and embossed with gold. Tall ladders lean against each shelf, stretching up to even more books above us.

"Oh, I could spend my whole life in here," I say, looking around at all the books. Even high above us, I can see floors and floors of other books, each with ornate balconies that look down into the empty space in the middle of the vast room.

"How many books do you think they have?" Ava asks.

"I couldn't even begin to guess. It would probably take a couple lifetimes to read them all," I say. I walk by one of the bookshelves and pick up the biggest book I see. It feels brand new as I gently open the cover. The language isn't one I know so I return it to the shelf.

We pass another android leaning against the end of one of the bookshelves, clutching a stack of books in her arms.

"Do you think the androids were running this place?" I say.

"What do you mean?" Ava asks.

"Like this one here with the books. I think she was a librarian," I say. "Same with the one at that front desk."

"That would make a lot of sense. It's pretty much what we use the androids for today," she says. I think back to the ones who carried our bags around June and helped out with everyday tasks around the city.

"It's sad they kind of just got left down here," I say, looking at the face of the librarian android in front of us. Hanging above her is a large oil painting with a golden plaque below it, just like the ones in the June library. I realize similar paintings also hang on the endcaps of all the other bookshelves around us.

"This one's pretty." I walk over to a different painting. It shows silhouettes of massive, towering trees standing over an old wooden cabin. The paint is thick and I can see the old impressions of the brushstrokes preserved in it. And yet, even though the paint is thick, there's still a few spots where the bare canvas peeks through.

"I wonder where that is," Ava says.

"It must be further south. I don't see a bit of snow anywhere," I say.

"The plaque here says 'Red Woods'." She points at the small metal plaque below the painting.

"Hm, never heard of it," I say.

"I'd love to go somewhere that warm." Ava stares longingly at the painting as I walk to the next one.

"Then I think you'll like this one too." It shows a vibrant city nestled on a cliffside. It sits next to a vast ocean, spotted with dozens of fancy-looking boats. Ava comes over and looks at it with me.

"Oh yeah, that one is really nice. You know, I've never actually seen a real body of water before."

"Really?"

"Yeah, just the ice sheet. I'd love to go somewhere like that." She points at the painting.

That's when I notice something near the edge of the painting.

"Wait, what's that?" I pull the painting off the wall and lay it on the ground to get a closer look.

"What is it?" Ava asks, looking closely at the detail of the painted city alongside me.

"That's the lighthouse. Wardenclyffe," I say, pointing at a white building on the cliffside.

"That can't be right." Ava stands up and looks at the plaque on the wall. "See, it says that city is Juneau." When she says it out loud, it clicks for both of us.

"June-au," I say.

"That can't be." Ava comes back to look at the painting.

"This must be before it froze."

"It used to be so beautiful. I wonder what happened to it."

"Well, whatever it was must have been from a lifetime ago." I lean the painting up against the wall.

"Wanna head back?" Ava asks.

"Yeah, it's probably gonna take us hours to get home," I say, thinking about all the climbing we have ahead of us. We start to walk back through the room towards the entrance when one painting in particular catches my eye. It's of a group of people standing in front of a massive metal vehicle.

"Wait, look at that!" I run up and point at one of the people in the painting.

"Is that—?"

"That's Saffron!" I exclaim. "What is she doing in that painting?"

"She looks exactly the same."

Ava's completely right. She has the exact same face and even the same red coat. I look at the date on the plaque below the painting. 2298, even before this place was sealed up.

"How could that be?" Ava asks.

Before I can answer, there's a voice from behind us.

"Well, it looks like you two figured it out," the voice says.

I slowly turn around and see Saffron standing behind us. She smiles and my stomach sinks. I grab Ava's hand and hold it tightly.

CHAPTER EIGHT

SAFFRON

"Hello, Olivia. Hello, Ava," she says.

I glance back at the painting of her on the wall. There's no mistake that it's absolutely her in the picture.

"What're you doing here?" I ask.

"You know, I could ask you the same question." She walks towards us. Her shoes clink loudly against the floor and echo throughout the room.

"What do you mean?" Ava asks.

"Well, you see, I've been trying to get inside here for a very, very long time. And yet somehow the two of you manage it within a few weeks." She stops just in front of us. "I want to know how you found your way to that entrance." She stares us down.

"Why would we tell you?" I say.

"I think you will. Either way, I had a hunch that if I followed you, you might lead me somewhere I hadn't found yet. Especially after I caught you exploring the sea caves."

"You weren't there," I say.

"A more accurate statement would be that you didn't see me there." She gives a very fake smile.

"How are you in that painting?" I ask.

"Yeah, that doesn't make any sense," Ava chimes in.

"You two really have no idea what you've gotten yourself into," she says.

"Then why don't you explain it to us?" Ava says.

"We really don't have time for that," Saffron says. "You two are going to come with me now," she continues, gesturing towards the door we came in through.

"Like hell we are!"

Saffron pulls something out of her coat that looks like a small pistol, although not like any I've seen before. "I'm afraid that wasn't a suggestion," she says, pointing the pistol at us.

"Oh, come on, what're you going to do with that?" I say sarcastically.

Saffron points the pistol upwards and pulls the trigger. The barrel lights up with a bright light before releasing a blinding white beam into the ceiling. The air crackles with electricity and the hairs on my arms stand up on end. Ava grabs onto my arm tightly and pulls me close as the tattered pages of books rain down around us.

"Now, I don't want to use this, but I will if I have to." She aims the pistol at us again.

"But what do you need us for?" I ask.

"You're going to help me get something I need. Now let's go." She gestures to the exit of the room again.

"It's gonna be ok," I whisper to Ava as we start walking.

We walk through the room with the artifacts on pedestals and back out into the large circular room with the broken statues. I glance around and look for any spot we might be able to escape to.

"Don't even think about it," Saffron says from behind us.

I turn back towards her and see the pistol still pointed directly at us. "What do you mean?"

"You're looking for a way to escape from me. But you're not quick enough, I can tell you that for sure. Now let's head back up." She gestures towards the spiraling ramp we followed to get down here. Ava and I keep walking, Saffron following a couple of paces behind.

"So why were you taking the power cells from the androids?" I ask as we walk past one of the androids laying in our path.

"It's not important," Saffron says, stepping over its body.

"Was it all just to get inside here? Trying to power up that door we found in the sea caves?" I remember how beat up the door had looked, with even the control panel destroyed.

"You're incorrect," she says. "I mean, I can tell you're pretty smart. But also dead wrong on that count."

We keep walking up the ramp in silence for another couple of minutes. Eventually we arrive at the balcony where we started. I look down over the statues one last time before Saffron ushers us back into the hallway.

She leads us through the room we had our picnic in and through one of the other doors off the room. It looks the same as the other hallways that we've been in. I can't imagine how people didn't get lost all the time in here. The hallway abruptly ends with a large bulkhead, next to which is a small black panel.

Saffron gestures to the panel with her pistol. "Put your hand there."

"Why?" Ava asks.

"Just do it."

I consider whether to do what she says but the pistol doesn't seem to be giving me much choice. I walk over and place my hand on the cold glass surface of the panel. It lights up brightly then makes a sudden 'ping'. As it does, the bulkhead door slowly rises.

The three of us step under the door and into a long room with a wall of windows that look down into another massive room, but unlike the first one, this one has a large ship right in the middle.

"It's a ship?" Ava asks.

"Let's keep moving." Saffron brushes off her question but my mind continues to race, trying to put everything together. We head down a set of stairs and out into the cavernous room.

The ship is a lot to take in. The whole thing looks like it's taken quite a beating, with some of its metal panels scattered across the floor nearby. Even from back here I can see large tendrils of orange crystal growing through the hull, whole areas where the panels have just been pushed aside. The crystals stretch throughout the room, even up to the ceiling, like a thick spiderweb that the ship got caught in.

I also notice more letters on the far wall of the room that say '*PHOEBE*' but there's a thick line painted through them and below, in a totally different style, it says '*ASTERIA*'. The same word is painted on the side of the ship.

"We're finally here," Saffron says.

"So does that mean we can go?" I ask hopefully.

"No, you're going to help me get in there." Saffron walks up to the side of the ship.

It's propped up by large metal supports, one of which has been completely engulfed by the orange crystal. We walk underneath it and I can see the dark metal of the ship closely. The whole surface is covered in scratches and dents, like someone threw a bunch of rocks at it.

From underneath the ship, it looks just as bad, more crystals growing through the metal, extending all the way to the floor of the room. I also can't see any kind of door to get inside.

"Over here." Saffron calls us over to one of the metal supports, where I notice a control board. We make eye contact and she nods towards a small black panel in the middle of the board. I place my hand on it and it lights up green with a 'ping', just like the one before. A loud grinding sounds from the back of the ship.

We rush over to where the noise is coming from to see the whole back wall lowering into a big ramp. Some orange crystals that had been near the hinges crack apart and fall to the floor. The ramp clangs to the ground and the motors that had been lowering it grind to a halt.

"Are you ok?" I whisper to Ava as I reach down to hold her hand.

"Yeah, just nervous," she says, but her expression betrays her. She looks terrified. I squeeze her hand tightly.

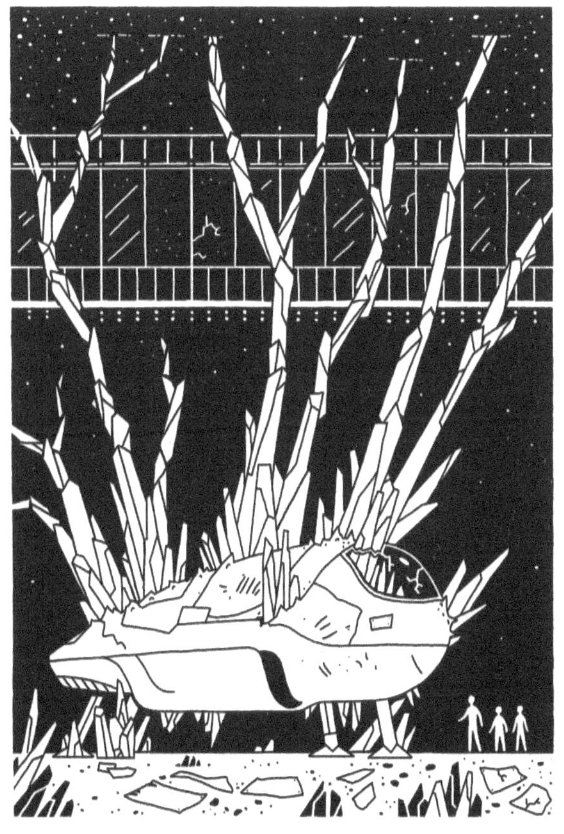

"We're gonna be fine," I tell her. I turn to Saffron. "What is this?"

"This is the *Asteria*," Saffron says, finally answering one of our questions.

"Yeah, but what is that?"

"It's a ship," she responds.

Talking to her feels like talking to a brick wall. I'm barely getting any information. "Yeah, I can see that much. But what was it for?"

"Not important," she responds.

We walk up the ramp into a pretty cramped hallway. The length of it is stocked with old boxes, which makes it feel more like a storage cabinet than any kind of ship. There's a couple of doors leading off the hallway, all open.

Ava and I duck into the first one. There are small cots set up in each corner and a dried-up plant laying on the ground next to a small, broken pot. Dead leaves lay scattered around the floor. I accidentally step on one and it crunches into dust beneath my foot.

"It looks like a bedroom," Ava says.

"Bit cramped for a bedroom."

Saffron appears in the doorway. "Let's keep moving." She ushers us into the hallway with all the boxes and kicks one over to us. "Start looking through these and let me know if you find anything."

"What're you looking for?" I ask.

"Just let me know if you find anything," she says.

"I'm just saying, might help us in the search if you told us what we're actually looking for," I say.

"Just look around." She paces up and down the hallway, looking over the piles of boxes and poking her head into some of the other rooms. She walks over to the wall, and grabs the corner of a metal panel, and effortlessly rips it off the wall. Just out of curiosity, I try pulling on one of the metal wall panels near me, but it doesn't budge. Just how strong is this woman?

"We should go out for dinner after this," I whisper to Ava.

"How can you think about dinner at a time like this?" she snaps.

"I'm hungry. We've been down here a while," I say, waiting for her reaction.

"You're ridiculous."

I look for a smile but her face remains stoic. Her entire demeanor shifted once we ran into Saffron.

"Be quiet, you two," Saffron says.

The boxes seem to be filled with random stuff. Some contain what look like tools, though I couldn't even begin to guess what they'd be used for. Another is filled with a bunch of tattered journals and loose papers.

One box is just a bunch of empty, clear containers.

"Here's something," I say, tossing Saffron one of the empty containers. She raises an eyebrow then quickly frowns.

"I'm not in the mood for jokes."

"Well, how do I know that's not what you're looking for?" I argue.

"Keep looking." She walks away.

"There's nothing here," I say. "Whatever you're looking for is probably long gone."

"No, it's here somewhere," Saffron says. That's when she seems to notice something at the end of the hallway. She kneels down, digging her fingers under a part of the wall. The wall moves and my jaw drops as she raises the bulkhead above her head. It blended in so well I didn't even realize there was a door there. She lets go, leaving deep impressions in the metal where her grip had been.

Beyond the door is another room filled with the orange crystal, clearly the source of where it's growing from.

"You can't really expect us to go in there," I say.

"Yes. And whatever you do, don't touch the crystal," Saffron says.

I look down at my bandaged hand. "Why shouldn't we touch it?" I ask, my voice shaking.

"Just don't, ok." She waves us into the room and I hug the back wall, making sure to stay as far away from the crystal as possible. Why shouldn't we touch them? What's going to happen to me since I did?

I get closer to the crystal and notice a faint red glow coming from inside, surrounded by a darker section of something, maybe another rock. It resembles the dark veins I had seen in other crystals, but this one is all concentrated in one spot.

"What is that?" The red light shimmers through the crystal, refracting bright red spots of light throughout the room.

"That is what I've been looking for," Saffron says. She walks up and places her hands onto the crystal.

"I thought you said not to touch it." I look at her hands against it.

"No, I told *you* not to touch it." She doesn't look back at us when she says this. Instead, she steps back and removes her coat. She's wearing a white shirt with long flowing sleeves and fancy tailored red pants. She doesn't look dressed for exploring at all. She starts to roll up the sleeves of her shirt.

"So now what?" I ask.

When she turns back to us, her expression looks completely different. "You two managed to find your way down here, so now you're going to help me get that thing out of there." She walks out into the hallway, grabs the box of weird tools, and brings it back over to us, dropping it onto the ground with a loud clang.

"But I thought you told us not to touch the crystal," Ava says.

"You won't. That's what those are for." Saffron points to the box of tools at my feet. I pick one of them up. It looks kind of like a garden spade, but with a bunch of extra machinery attached to the handle.

I flip it around in my hands. "How does this even work?"

"Well, not like that." Saffron walks over and grabs it from me. "This part goes forward, and then you pull this to turn it on." She moves my hand over a switch on the side of the tool. I press the switch and the long end begins to vibrate rapidly.

"What are all these?" I move the tool back and forth and it makes a noticeable humming noise.

"Geological survey equipment."

"How did you know it was here?" I look at the other tools in the old cardboard box.

"Not important," she says.

"Of course it is." I point the end of the tool at her intimidatingly. "How were you in that painting?"

"It's not important." She's completely unfazed by the tool in her face.

"Like hell it's not!" I say. "You've been up to something for a while now. You followed us here, you knew about this weird ship and all the tools on it and whatever that is." I gesture to the glowing object within the crystal. "And not to mention whatever you're doing taking the power cells out of all the androids in June." I'm a little bit out of breath after my tirade.

"Look, all I want is that thing in there. Once you help me get it out, we can all go our separate ways." She suddenly moves lightning fast and grabs the tool out of my hand, then turns around and thrusts it into the crystal. When she does, there's a loud crack and the crystal fractures. I can see dozens of cracks running throughout it now. Ava picks up one of the other tools.

"What're you doing?" I ask her.

"I just wanna get out of here," she says. "I figure the sooner we get that thing out, the sooner we'll be able to leave." She digs the tool into the crystal and it seems to slice through it with ease. She slices off a large piece and I can feel the frustration radiating off her as she works. I look back at Saffron, who's busy cutting the crystal apart.

"Ugh fine." I pick up another one of the tools and start helping the two of them. "But I want it on record that this is an extremely stupid idea."

The three of us continue to cut into the large crystal structure. It's an awkward process and both Ava and I are careful not to actually touch any of the crystals. Saffron picks up the larger pieces and moves them out of the way. It was hard to tell when we first started but the crystal structure is much thicker than I was expecting, at least eight feet thick.

I pause from carving and look around the room for a bit. The crystal structure takes up most of the space, but I can still see light filtering in from outside. And just based on the layout, this feels like it would be the bridge of the ship. I still have to wonder what it was originally used for.

"Stand back." I turn back and Saffron is standing in front of the crystal with a small glowing cylinder in her hand. She places it onto the part of the crystal we've dug into the most. I step back and Ava stands behind me. Saffron presses a button on the cylinder and retreats. There's a bright flash of light and the crystal shatters inward.

"What was that?" I look around at the crystal dust now coating the floor.

"Mining charge," Saffron says. She steps into the space where the crystal used to be. All that remains is the darker mineral and, protruding from it, the object that's producing the red glow. It's a small, hexagonal object about the size of my hand, and in the center there's a bright red glow. The darker stone is wrapped around the object but not enough to hide any of the details.

"Finally. After all this time." Saffron reaches for the glowing object, but the second her fingers touch it, she's thrown backwards across the room into the metal wall and collapses to the floor. There's a pulse of red light from the object and I run to Saffron's side, Ava close behind me. She stirs but looks like she's in rough shape, the wall behind her dented from where she was thrown into it.

"How are you still moving?" I ask.

Saffron looks up at us. "I'm more durable than you'd think."

"No, she's right. Being thrown into a wall like that would be enough to kill anyone. How did you survive?" Ava asks.

Saffron reaches up towards the pulsing red light and that's when I get a clear look at her arm. There's a deep gash running from her hand all the way up to her elbow, but beneath her skin is not flesh and blood, but rather metal and sparking wires.

"You're an android," I say with disbelief.

"Insightful as always, Olivia," Saffron says.

I grab her hand and look at the wiring inside. It's some of the most advanced-looking circuitry I've ever seen.

"How is that even possible?" Ava asks.

"It's a long story," Saffron says, "but suffice to say, I've been trying to get in here a very long time." She tries to sit herself up with her other arm, but it doesn't look like her body is responding. Her legs are completely bent out of shape and where her knee used to be, I can see pieces of metal poking through the fabric of her pants.

"But why? What was so important in here?" I ask.

She reaches out to the glowing red object as it pulses again. "I need that power cell," she says.

"Wait, it's a power cell?"

"Unlike any other in the world."

I take a step back and trip over something in her red coat. I reach into the pockets and pull out a bundle of the android power cells, along with a bunch of crumpled papers.

"But why have you been taking these?" I hold the glowing power cells up in front of her. She reaches down and opens the panel in her chest, and I see four power cells, their glow dim, almost completely out.

"All the power cells out there are reaching the end of their life. I didn't have any other options," she says.

I ponder this as I unfold the papers and read them over. *User Manual TR076 - Unreleased.* That sounds so familiar for some reason. "Oh wait, you tore these out of the book in the library. Why?"

"Just in case anyone started poking around too much." She looks directly at me when she says this.

Ava grabs the papers from me, flipping through them. She suddenly stops and holds a page up. "That's her." On the page Ava's holding up, there's a drawing of Saffron.

"So that was your user manual?" I ask.

"Not that it really matters anymore, but yes," Saffron says.

"But you seem so real," Ava says.

"Well, I am real." Saffron sounds offended.

"But you're not human," I say.

"No, but that doesn't make me not real."

"What I mean is that you seem like you're an actual person. All the other androids aren't anywhere close," I say.

Saffron sighs. "Do you know what AI is?"

"Yeah, we learned about it in school. It was that thing for computers, right?" I ask Ava.

"For, like, navigation I think," she confirms.

"It's a lot more than that. The AI frameworks allow a computer to actually learn new things and make its own decisions. At first, it'll seem just like a normal machine, but after a while it's just like it's really alive," she explains.

"So what's that have to do with you?" Ava asks.

Saffron stares at me and it clicks. "You're an AI?" I ask.

"And another point for Olivia," she says sarcastically.

"I've never heard of an android with an AI system before," Ava says.

"I was a prototype version. But there was a huge backlash against adding AI into androids, so they shut the program down, leaving just me. And once the colony ships launched, the idea of using AI pretty much shut down completely." As she continues to talk, there's a static noise coming from her voice.

"The colony ships? What are you talking about?" I ask.

"You were dozing off in that class," Ava whispers to me before turning to Saffron. "But that was long before even the flooding happened."

"Yes, it was," Saffron says. Her speaking sounds much slower now

"But that would make you hundreds of years old!" I say.

"That is correct," she says, her voice continuing to slow down.

"How have you been going for so long?"

"Well, it's mainly—" She stops talking, her face completely frozen.

"Saffron?" I wave my hand in front of her face but there's no reaction.

"What happened to her?" Ava asks.

"I have an idea about that." I reach down and remove the old power cells from the panel in her chest and swap in the ones from her coat. They click into place and she suddenly jolts back to life.

"—been by replacing my…" She stops mid-sentence and looks down at the open panel on her chest. "Well, looks like you've figured that part out too." She reaches up with her only working hand and closes the panel.

The red light from the object suddenly begins to pulse even brighter, refracting through the remaining crystal structures surrounding it. As it does, hundreds of tiny lights suddenly turn on throughout the room and the ship shakes violently as something whirrs to life.

"What's it doing?" I stand up. Suddenly there's a ping and a voice rings throughout the ship.

"Attention. Launch sequence initiated. All crew members to your designated jump seats," the voice says.

"If you two know what's good for you, you'll get out of here," Saffron says.

"Why would we go?" I ask.

The voice echoes throughout the ship again. "Launch to commence in fifteen minutes."

"This ship has an engine with enough power to punch a hole in space. When it boots up, it's going to vaporize anything nearby," Saffron says.

Ava tugs at my arm. "Let's run."

"But what about you?" I look over at Saffron laying on the ground, her metal limbs twisted out of shape.

"Oh, kid, take a look at me. There aren't enough parts in the world to put me back together," she says.

Ava tugs at my arm again, completely panicked. "We gotta get out of here."

"We can't just leave her!"

"Why not? She's the one that kidnapped us!"

"That doesn't mean we should just leave her to die!" I pull away from Ava and run to Saffron's side. I lean down and try to lift her up.

"You can't lift me," Saffron says.

"Just watch me." I pull harder to try and lift her from the ground but she doesn't budge.

"Olivia, come on!" Ava yells from across the room.

"I'm solid metal. You'd have to be an android yourself to lift that much on your own." Saffron places her hand on my cheek. "No one lives forever." There's a tear coming from her eye.

Ava runs over and pulls me away from her. I turn away and run out of the room with her, glancing back one more time to look at Saffron. She gives me one last wink before we're gone.

"We have to get out of here," Ava says, looking panicked.

"This way." I lead her back down the ramp at the back of the ship.

"Ship launch sequence beginning in ten minutes," says the automated voice, ringing out through the ship as we manage to make it outside. But outside the ship we're over-whelmed by a loud roar coming from the engines.

"That doesn't sound good." I run to get a better view of them and both have a bright red glow. I can feel the heat on my face even from this far away.

"Those must be the engines. We need to leave now," Ava says.

As they continue to heat up, I feel them start to pulse through the room. The air vibrates around us.

"Agreed." I nod and look around the room. There's a spiral staircase in the corner that looks like the one we had climbed down in in the first room. I point to it. "Over there."

"Let's go."

As Ava and I run over to the staircase, I feel around my shoulder.

"My bag is gone," I say.

"We don't have time to go back for it," Ava says, already up a couple of steps. The roar of the engines is getting even louder now.

"Damn, I really liked that bag too." I follow her onto the steps and we both run up them as fast as we possibly can. I look down at the ship from above as we climb. It's unlike anything I've ever seen before, the design completely foreign. We eventually reach the top of the staircase and come to another door.

"It's closed," Ava says, a clear panic in her voice.

"Wait, look at that!" There's a small lever near the side of the door that reads 'EMER-GENCY RELEASE'.

"Well, if this isn't an emergency then I don't know what is." Ava reaches up and pulls the lever. There's a rush of air and the door springs open forcefully. We climb out of the staircase back into the bright, snowy land-scape above.

We manage to get a few steps away from the door when there's a massive pulse from below, which knocks us to the ground. As everything around us shakes violently, my ears ring from the sheer volume. There's a blast of flame from the door behind us and I feel the heat against my skin. The air in my lungs feels like it's vibrating. Ava and I hold each other close and wait for it to pass. The explosion seems to continue for an eternity until it suddenly stops and everything is quiet.

I let go of Ava and we both stand up and look around. All the snow surrounding us is completely melted and little green plants sit in muddy puddles. On the horizon there's a plume of dark black smoke rising.

"Isn't that…?" I start to say.

"That's where June is," she says.

We stare at the black smoke on the horizon with complete horror.

CHAPTER NINE

PANDEMONIUM

The two of us take off running towards June. My feet splash loudly in the muddy ground and the cold wind bites at my face, but with the pit in my stomach I can barely even process the cold. I've never seen Ava run this fast before. She's actually a lot faster than I am. After all the running and climbing the stairs, I'm completely exhausted but I push on.

"We're almost there," she yells back to me. The wooden gate is in the distance. I stick to the dirt part of the ground. A thick cloud of black smoke hangs above the entire city, blocking out most of the sunlight, making it feel like night.

Ava reaches the gate before me and stops in her tracks. I arrive and look out over the city. The buildings that used to make up the lower half are completely destroyed, their charred debris scattered across the ice shelf for what looks like miles. Massive fires roar in the places where the buildings used to be and plumes of smoke rise from them.

"What have we done?" Ava asks.

"This wasn't us!"

"Of course it was!" she yells. There are tears in her eyes as she starts to run down the steps. The entire city has erupted in pandemonium. The further we go, the worse the destruction gets. I stop at the street where the library used to be.

"The library is gone."

Ava stops next to me and looks at the wreckage. Where the library used to sit is now nothing more than a charred patch of ground. Not a single piece remaining. If I had to guess, the pieces are probably scattered across the ice shelf with the rest of the city.

"How is this even possible?" she asks.

"It must've been that ship, right?" I say. "I can't believe it could do something like this."

I look around more. It's just so much destruction for one ship. As we reach the lower levels, even fewer buildings remain intact. The cobblestone streets are still there, and the large stone steps, but that's about it. The remaining buildings are almost fully destroyed; most are just burnt wooden frames and others are still on fire.

"It's all gone," Ava says. She stops and just stares at the fires around us. I stand next to her, coughing as I try to avoid inhaling the smoke. There are still people running around in a panic. I see an android lying on the ground with his face completely melted off and his metal body charred and twisted out of shape.

We run down to the lowest level and find absolutely nothing left. All the docks are gone. There's part of a bus left but even the metal of its treads is completely melted away. But perhaps the most surprising sight is that the ice shelf has melted through, leaving a deep blue ocean in its place. It splashes up onto the stone walls below.

We run along the street, looking at the damage around us.

"The school is gone too," Ava says when we reach the end. And sure enough, the courtyard where our school used to sit is completely gone. Instead, there's a large smoking crater. I step over the rim and notice a series of large holes in the ground. I look inside the nearest one to find a deep tunnel with metal walls that have been burnt black by the fire.

I realize what I'm looking at. "Oh my god."

"What is it?" Ava looks concerned as I pull the map out of my jacket pocket.

"This was one of the tunnels." I point to the map. "It was all connected. When that

ship exploded, the explosion must have travelled through all the tunnels connected to where the ship was." I drop the map onto the ground and we look back up at the city together.

"So it really was our fault," Ava says.

"No! Saffron was the one that was messing around with that ship!" I remind her.

"But we helped her!"

"She would have done it whether or not we were there," I say.

"She never would have gotten into the ship without us!"

"You can't blame us for this!"

"Do you really think the city will see it that way?" she continues to yell.

"We were just exploring."

"I can't believe I let you drag me into this." She starts to run back towards the city. I go after her but she stops me. "Don't follow me. I can't deal with this right now."

"Deal with what?"

"With this! It's just too much!" She looks so angry with me. "Now I have to go make sure my family is still alive. I suggest you do the same." She turns away from me and runs back towards her house.

I stand there in shock. Her words echo in my head and suddenly I find myself running back up the stone steps towards where my house is. I have to make sure my parents are ok too.

Despite the streets being full of panicked people running around, I barely notice them as I run, even though I definitely end up running full-on into a lot of them on the way. But with the chaos, they don't seem to notice anyways. I get back up to the part of the city that has buildings again and start looking for my street.

It was much easier to navigate when things were calmer. The chaos has really thrown off the little sense of direction I had. I look around the street with panic. Every single building around here looks the same. Why couldn't they have been more creative with their architecture?

Suddenly a hand grabs my coat and pulls me backwards. I struggle and try to pull away until I hear, "Olivia!" The voice is loud and familiar. I stop struggling and turn around to see my mom grabbing the collar of my coat. A wave of relief washes over me and I give her the biggest hug. She holds me tight and the chaos around us seems to melt away a little bit. "I've been looking everywhere for you." There are tears in her eyes.

"I was trying to find our house." I can hear my voice crack, and my face is wet from tears too.

She grabs my hand and pulls me quickly down the street. "Let's get back home. It's not safe to be out here right now," she says. We run together until I finally see our house, miraculously still standing. I'm still in a complete panic but definitely relived it's still there.

"I thought you were dead," she says once we get inside. She holds me close and we stand there together in the living room. For some reason, all the lights are off.

"Why would you think that?" I ask through her embrace.

"I thought you and Ava had gone down to that gallery in the lower city," she says. Oh yeah, was it really only this morning she told me about that?

"Oh, no, we weren't there," I say.

"Well how would I have known that?" she snaps. "That whole part of town was vaporized." She doesn't let me go.

"But I'm ok. I wasn't there," I reassure her.

"We were absolutely worried sick," she says.

I pull away and look around the room. "Where's Dad?"

"He's trying to help the relief teams," she says, finally letting me out of her embrace. "He came to check in with me before heading back down."

"What relief teams?" I ask. "What can we do about the fires?" I imagine they just have to burn themselves out at this point.

"No, the fire crews will handle those. He's working on the power," she says.

I look around the room at all the lights that are currently off. "What happened to the power?"

"Whatever that explosion was completely knocked out power to the entire city. They're working to try and get it reconnected again," she says.

"Where is he now?"

"He's probably over at the lighthouse," she says. I run for the door but she grabs me by the back of my collar. "Where do you think you're going?" she yells.

"I need to talk to him."

She holds my collar tight. "No, you're staying right here until all of this is over."

"I have to see him right now." I slip out of the sleeves of my coat and bolt for the door. I rush outside and start running.

"OLIVIA, YOU COME BACK HERE THIS INSTANT," she yells after me. I keep running back down the streets until I see the lighthouse in the distance, then I sprint as fast as I can towards it. The air is unbearable without my jacket but I have to tell Dad about what we found. I run up to the door of the lighthouse and bang on it with my fists.

The door swings open and my dad is standing there. He looks a complete mess, hair all out of order, glasses cracked, and absolutely covered in thick black soot. He has a smell of burning wood to him.

"Olive?" He looks shocked. "Where have you been?" He pulls me into an embrace and walks me into the building. There are a bunch of other people standing around the first floor of the lighthouse with him. The only one I recognize is Kai but all the rest I've never seen before.

"I need to tell you something, right now," I say, low enough that the others can't hear us.

"But where were you? Your mom has been looking everywhere," he continues.

"I have to tell you this." I feel the eyes of everyone looking at us. "In private," I say, quieter.

"Ok, but we have to be quick." He leads me to the stairs and we climb up to the second floor, away from the crowd of strangers below.

"It's my fault," I say.

"What's your fault?" He seems confused and still a little distracted.

"That explosion. I know what caused it."

"How could you possibly know something like that?"

"Because I was there," I say.

He looks at me for a long time before speaking again. "I'm going to need way more information than that." He rubs his eyes. I don't think I've seen him look this tired in a long time.

"We've been exploring the tunnels around the city. I was kind of just curious about what they were."

He holds up a hand and stops me. "Who's 'we'?"

"Me and Ava. We found tunnels all over, like in the library, the school, the caves north of here. And they were all connected to this big underground facility. Plus, that woman Saffron was actually an android who was hundreds of years old and was stealing power cells from all the other androids in the city. And we found an old spaceship and, like, a weird museum full of old artifacts and a weird orange crystal growing everywhere." I stop for a breath and my dad just stares at me.

"You understand how ridiculous all that sounds," he says.

"Wait, I have proof." I pull the holo-recorder off my neck and swap out the disc for one of the others. "I think it was this one." I press play and it shows the view from the top of the lighthouse. "No, wait, give me a second." I open the cover and swap the disc to one of the others. I press play and the

holographic image of the giant statues appears above the holo-recorder.

"What is this?" He walks over and examines the recording carefully.

"I told you, it's the underground facility
we found," I say.

He reaches over and turns a knob on the
holo-recorder. The image of the statues grows
until they're about the size of a real person
and I can make out all of the details on them,
every crack and overgrown vine. I didn't even
know the recorder could zoom in like that
until now.

"Where is this?" He walks through the
recording, passing through the statues.

"It was underneath June," I say.

"What do you mean 'was'?"

"I think the explosion destroyed it."

"And what was the explosion?"

"It was that old spaceship we found. Or
Saffron found."

"How did she know about it?"

"She was hundreds of years old. She
knew about it from when the facility was still
active. But the whole place was sealed up
way before the flooding."

"Ok, that raises about a million more
questions but the most important is, probably,
what was the actual explosion?" He reaches
over again and turns off the holo-recording.

"Oh, yeah, so Saffron accidentally activated the launch sequence of the ship by grabbing some red glowing thing. I think she said it was some kind of power cell. And then the ship kind of exploded."

"Are you sure she said it was a power cell? How did it have enough force to cause all that damage to the city?"

"I'm not exactly sure, there was a lot going on. But whatever it was, it seemed pretty powerful the way she was talking about it."

He looks at me intensely. "Saffron?"

"There was a painting of her down in the facility. The facility was named Wardenclyffe too."

"What did you just say?" he whispers.

"The Wardenclyffe Institute. That's what the signs said," I say.

He shushes me, opens the top of the holo-recorder and slips the disc into his pocket. "Whatever you do, please keep that to yourself." He still seems completely panicked, and now I'm the confused one.

"But why?" I ask.

"Because that whole institute is a myth. Like Atlantis. No one thought it was real. I need time to look into this quietly and safely," he says. "And I don't want you seeing Ava again."

"Wait, that's not fair!" I argue.

"You've been getting into way more trouble than I realized with her. I can't have you running around the city like that anymore. Until further notice, you're grounded," he says sternly. He walks me back down the stairs into the room of other people, who still seem to be quietly discussing things among themselves.

"Where'd you run off to, Desmond?" one of them asks.

"Just going to bring Olivia here back home. Then I'll be back in a little bit." He gives me his coat and walks me outside. He escorts me back towards our house where I have a feeling I'm about to be spending a lot more of my time. The destruction of the city around us haunts me as we walk past.

◆

I roll over out of bed. It feels like I've been trapped in my room for ages. This whole grounding thing is starting to get old. Not that there's really much else to do right now; even school's been on hold since the entire building is gone.

I walk over to the window and look out at the streets below. Everything is completely quiet, the vibrancy of the city dimmed by the devastation. I think most everyone is still in shock, trying to figure out how we're going to rebuild. It's been almost a week since I've seen Ava, but hopefully that will change soon.

I walk over to my closet and pull out my clothes for the day. My arm feels stiff as I reach up to the hangers. I catch a whiff of smoke from some of the clothes hanging there. Even after a couple of days and some washing the smoke smell still hasn't faded from them, although it's hard to be sure if it's from them, or just lingering smells of burning from the rest of the city. I change into some other clothes instead and make my way downstairs.

There's a big fire in the fireplace; the heat from it has been enough to keep the house pretty warm throughout the day.

Mom is sitting on the large sofa in front of the fire. "Good morning, sweetie," she says.

I sit down next to her. "Hey." I can feel the heat from the fire against my face and the warmth makes me want to just curl up and stay in the house all day.

She wraps her arm around me. "You gonna go help your dad today?"

"I mean, it's the only thing I'm allowed to do right now," I say.

"You know why we had to ground you, right?"

"Yeah."

"Look, you've been getting into dangerous stuff. We need to know you're safe. Especially with the city the way it is now. Everything's still in complete turmoil."

I don't respond but I snuggle closer to her. I look into the kitchen and see all the appliances are gone. "You got rid of all the electronics," I point out.

"Not much use for them without electricity," she says.

"So, what're we going to do?"

"Well, you're gonna go help your dad over at the lighthouse."

I pull away from her. "No, I mean, like, can we even live here without electricity?"

"Some people don't think we can." She shakes her head.

"But what about you?"

"I honestly don't know. Another bus is taking people south this afternoon. I keep wondering if it would be better if we went back to University."

"You'd really leave just like that? Dad too?"

"Well, that's where we have slightly different opinions. I think it's going to take a lot to drag your dad away from this place."

"And what about you?"

"Probably a bit less to get me away from here. I miss the warm weather. And I feel like the city is about to get a lot quieter."

"What do you mean?"

"A lot of people are leaving. More buses are coming every day. People lost their friends, loved ones, even homes, and others are concerned about living without the connection to the grid."

"So they're just gonna go?"

"It's their choice to leave. But I also understand it. I can already feel the city changing." She looks up at the clock. "You should probably get ready to go. Your dad's expecting you soon," she continues.

I get up from the sofa and she walks over to the kitchen. She comes back with something wrapped in cloth.

"What's this?" I look at it closely.

"Just some breakfast. It's not as fancy as what I could make in the kitchen, but we might have to get used to cooking without it for a bit."

"I'm sure it's wonderful," I say. I grab my coat and give my mom a big hug before opening the front door.

"And remember, straight to the lighthouse," she says as I leave.

There's a lump in the pocket of the coat. I reach in and pull out the holo-recorder, still with the string I tied around it. I hold it in my hands as I walk through the city. The devastation is heartbreaking. Half the city just gone in an instant, all those people dead. I try to tell myself it's not my fault, but the guilt is eating away at me.

I walk down to one of the lower streets and aim the holo-recorder and face it down the street, flipping the switch to turn it on. "So, we got in a bit of trouble last week," I say. The buildings on this street are mostly intact, so it's not immediately clear what happened. "We found this cool, abandoned place and went out to explore it." I pause, thinking back to the institute. "But some stuff happened that wasn't too great. I don't want to get into all that right now." I hear my voice break. I thought it would be good to record what happened but I'm not sure if I actually can.

"I told my dad about what we found and he kind of freaked out. He says I'm not allowed to see Ava anymore," I say, turning onto the stone stairs and walking down to the next level. "I'm still going to, obviously. But something about the place we went really freaked Dad out."

As I'm walking along the street, I look at the burned-out buildings around me. Some wooden structures still remain but they're all charred and black now.

A fresh layer of snow sits on top of them, hiding some of the destruction. The part of the ice shelf that had melted has frozen over again, now with bits of debris sticking out of the ice. There had been some teams trying to retrieve the debris, but I think most have given up on that effort now that it's all frozen again. I turn onto the street with Wardenclyffe at the end and point the holo-recorder directly at it.

"I think he was talking about moving his lab up there," I say, recalling a whispered conversation I overheard between him and Kai the other night. I stare up at the lighthouse in front of me before stepping inside. The room is probably the messiest I've ever seen it, just junk littered around everywhere. "So I think I'll take this place over once he moves all this crap out of here," I joke into the holo-recorder.

I hear footsteps coming and slip the holo-recorder into my pocket again. I'm not sure my dad would want me to be recording stuff right now, even though it was his idea in the first place.

Unlike the last time I was here, there's not a large crowd of people, just my dad and Kai walking down the staircase from the floor above. With the electricity gone, the only light comes from the fireplace on the opposite side of the room and the slivers of light coming in through the narrow windows.

"Where's everyone else?" I ask.

"Gone," my dad says. He sounds frustrated.

"Are they coming back?"

"It doesn't seem likely." Kai comes over and gives me a hug.

"Why not?"

"Most of them left June this morning," she says.

"But not you?"

She smiles. "I've spent my whole life in this city. I don't see any reason to abandon ship now."

My dad is busy tinkering with another machine on his worktable. I walk over and stand next to him.

"How's the new power cell coming along?" I ask him.

"Poorly," he responds.

"What're you trying this time?"

"We're trying some of the crystals Kai was studying," he explains. Kai comes over carrying a clear box with the orange crystals in it. The exact same crystals that were growing down in the underground city and the spaceship.

"Are you sure those are safe?" I ask, thinking of Saffron's warning.

"For the most part. They're hard to handle but apart from that they've been a great power source," she explains.

"What do you mean they're hard to handle?" I ask, my palm still numb from where it was cut by the crystal.

"Well, when I was running tests on them, I found that they would begin to crystalize any organic matter they came into contact with," she says, and my heart sinks. Saffron warned us. She knew. I try to push aside my thoughts about what's going to happen to my hand. It's probably fine.

I turn back to my dad. "So how's it working?"

"There's a lot of power in them but we can't seem to harness that power for any kind of extended period. Just short bursts of energy," he says.

"What does that mean for the power cell?" I look over the machine on the table.

"That it'll be very effective for about ten minutes before burning out."

"We're looking at some other options, though," Kai adds.

"Nothing promising," my dad says. He walks over to another table with a machine on it. It seems like every table has a completely different machine, each one with wires coming off it and running up the walls. He flips a switch on one and it roars to life, rattling loudly.

"We'll see what this one gives us," Kai says, walking over to join my dad. As the machine whirrs, the lights inside of the room slowly light up. There's an orange glow coming from inside of the machine.

"What's powering that one?" I ask.

"Power cells from an android," Dad says.

"You just took them from them?" I say.

"Of course we did. I needed power and they had some," he responds.

"But is that right?"

"What're you talking about?"

"You just deactivate them because we need power?"

"They're not alive, dear," Kai says.

"But are we sure?" I think of Saffron. I know she said she was the only android with AI but something about just deactivating all of them feels wrong to me.

"Look, this is more important. Getting power back has to be our priority," Dad says. Suddenly there's a pulse of light and the machine shuts down. The lights in the room dim as it stops. He turns to Kai. "How long was that one?"

"About two minutes," she says.

"So practically nothing."

"Isn't that at least a little good?" I chime in.

"Two minutes and it barely powered the lights in this room. There's no way something like that will even come close to powering the whole city." I can feel his frustration as he slumps into one of the chairs, head in his hands.

Kai leans in and whispers to him, "What about what you mentioned the other night?"

"I don't think we have any other choice about that now."

"What're you talking about?" I ask.

"I told Kai about the Wardenclyffe Institute," he says.

"Wait, why?" I yell.

"I need that power cell that Saffron was looking for," he says bluntly.

"Why would you want anything like that?"

"Because anything that has that much power is our best shot for bringing power back to the city."

"What if it was destroyed?" I ask.

"We're just going to have to take that chance."

"I'm not going back down there."

"No, of course you're not. You're going to stay home and not get involved with this anymore." He stands up from his chair. "Grab your coat. I'm going to bring you back home to your mother." He turns to Kai. "Northern gate. One hour."

She nods.

He walks me out of the lighthouse and closes the door behind us. We walk back towards June in silence. Ever since I told him about what happened in the institute, he's been more distant. Distracted, too. We get closer to the city and from this direction the destruction looks even worse.

"You're really going up there?" I ask.

"I am."

"Are you sure?"

"Of course I am." He doesn't look at me.

"It's dangerous," I say, and he looks out over the city.

"Clearly."

I can tell he's not feeling big on talking right now but I try one more time to warn him. "Saffron was killed when she tried to touch that power cell."

He doesn't react, so I drop the conversation and continue to walk back with him to the house quietly. We walk inside and Mom greets us.

"Didn't expect to see the two of you so soon!" she says.

"Olive's going to stay here. Kai and are going up north again," Dad says.

"Oh?"

"Might be gone a while." He leans in and gives her a kiss before quickly leaving.

Mom stands in the doorway. "He's so different lately," she says.

"Yeah."

"It's like he feels like it's his responsibility to fix everything in the city. I honestly don't know why, though," she says. I feel a pit in my stomach. Is he trying to make up for what I did? She seems to notice the look on my face and quickly changes the topic. "You know what, let's get some food going." I walk over to the kitchen with her and try to get my head back into reality.

"What're we making?" I ask.

"Stew." She starts pulling things out of the cupboards.

"Why stew?" I ask. We haven't had that for ages.

"Well, it's something we can make over the fire." She pulls out a massive black pot with an oversized handle and a large iron pan. She continues to pull out a couple of ingredients from the shelves. "Plus, we need to use most of these before they go bad," she says.

I help her prep the food in the kitchen before she brings it over to the fire and starts cooking some of the meat we have. She calls out for various things from the kitchen, which I bring over to her and she tosses into the iron pan. After a couple of minutes, she hangs the large black pot over the flame and begins to add all the ingredients. She stirs it with a large wooden spoon. The smell of the spices and herbs fill the room.

"That smells incredible."

"Yeah, it's the last of our good spices," she says.

"What're we going to do after this?"

"Well, we're going to keep this going for a while. We can keep adding meat and vegetables to it as we need," she explains. She walks over to one of the chairs and sits down facing the fire.

"So now what?" I sit down in a chair near her.

"Now we wait for it all to cook."

I listen to the stew inside the pot bubble slowly. She occasionally gets up and stirs it. Neither of us seem to be in the talking mood tonight. I watch the flames dance around, and after a couple of hours, the sun goes down and light no longer comes through the windows. The only illumination now is from the fireplace as it casts long shadows throughout the room.

Mom grabs two wooden bowls and scoops large portions of the stew into each one, filling them to the brim. She hands me my bowl and a spoon. I dig in and am instantly overwhelmed by the taste of everything together. Somehow, even with all the different ingredients, everything blends perfectly and warms my body as I eat.

But the spoon feels awkward in my hand. My fingers are stiff and there's still a pain in my palm from where I cut it on the crystal. There's a pit in my stomach every time I think about it. It's been a week; shouldn't it be feeling better by now? Maybe it's an infection, and nothing as bad as Kai made out. I try to push those thoughts down as I shovel more of the stew into my mouth.

We both finish our food. After clearing up, I give Mom a hug and make my way back upstairs to my room. She's been sleeping in the living room the past few days on the big sofa so she can tend to the fire and keep it burning. The hallway is cold but luckily my room is still pretty warm. I lay in my bed, fully clothed, and stare at the ceiling. I miss Ava.

I still haven't seen her since we got back to June. I wonder if she's been thinking about me. I hold my hand up to my chest. I wish I could feel her hand in mine again. We left things in such a bad place the last time we spoke.

I look out the window and see a bunch of snow falling softly. I get up and walk over to the window to watch it. The city is dimly lit by moonlight but all the lights that used to be around are still completely out.

I wait a couple more minutes before walking over to my closet, grabbing one of my thick coats, and pulling it on over my outfit. I carefully hang the holo-recorder around my neck again and make my way over to the window. When I push it open, a cool breeze fills the room. I climb out onto the balcony and shut the window tightly behind me. Don't want that cold breeze blowing through the house.

I climb over one of the railings and dangle down off the side. It's not too far up. I feel around for a spot to put my foot but don't find any good ones. My grip starts to slip and before I can pull myself up, I'm falling. I land with a soft thud in the powdery snow. It may have softened the fall but not by too much.

I pull myself up and start walking along the street towards Ava's house. Hopefully I can sneak up to her window and see how she's doing. As I'm walking, I'm caught completely by surprise, seeing Ava walking along the street nearby. She's far away but we make eye contact. Or at least, I think we do. She turns away and keeps walking. Maybe she didn't actually see me. I run after her, the holo-recorder bouncing into my chest as I go.

"Ava, wait up!" I call after her. She starts running too. Ok, she definitely saw me, but I just want to talk to her. I finally catch up and she turns back to me. There are tears in her eyes. I hear the holo-recorder make a soft beep to let me know the disc is full. Was it recording that?

"What do you want?" she asks, clearly upset.

"I wanted to see you. It's been like over a week." I'm completely out of breath after running.

"I told you it was too much for me," she says.

"Wait, what was too much for you?"

"Our relationship."

"I thought you meant everything getting destroyed," I say. What does she mean our relationship?

"It's all the same thing! Being with you is more than I can handle." She sounds completely choked up. This is worse than I realized. "You just kept pushing to do crazier and crazier things. I would've been happy just staying at home and reading, but no, you had to keep pushing us to do more dangerous stuff. It was only a matter of time until something like this happened."

"I thought you were having fun!"

"I was fun at first, but you didn't listen when I started to get uncomfortable."

"I thought you were just joking around. It seemed like you needed to get out of your comfort zone a little," I say.

Her eyes narrow. "What does that mean?"

"You just seemed a little closed-off when I got here."

"It's not your job to fix me," she says.

"I wasn't trying to fix you! I just thought —"

"No. You didn't think," she cuts me off. "But I'm done, ok?"

"Wait, so what does that mean?" I feel the pit in my stomach as I ask the question.

"I'm breaking up with you. And I don't want to see you again." She turns away from me.

"Ava, please, no." My voice breaks. She doesn't look back as she walks away. Tears roll down my cheeks as I watch her go and my chest feels like it's just been ripped open. I stand there in the middle of the street, letting my tears freeze on my face.

CHAPTER TEN

EDELWEISS

I don't remember getting home. Did I walk back? And what about my mom? I think she talked to me. Or did she yell at me? Everything is a little fuzzy. It's light outside now and I'm lying in my bed again. I curl up in the large blanket and pull it tightly over my head to block out the light in the room. All my energy is completely gone and my chest feels tight. I hear the door to my room open. Someone sits down on the bed next to where I'm curled up and puts their hand on my back.

"Are you ok, sweetie?" I hear my mom's voice from outside the blanket.

"No." I can't seem to stop crying.

"What happened?"

"Ava broke up with me," I say.

"Oh, I'm so sorry, Olive." She rubs my back through the blanket. "I know how much you liked her."

"She said it was all just too much."

"You know, this whole ordeal was very traumatic for a lot of people. Maybe after a bit of space things might be better."

"She says she doesn't want to see me anymore." I can't get the image out of my head of her standing there telling me that.

"Well, you can't make her see you if she doesn't want to."

"But why not?"

"Because that's not what she wants right now. And maybe that'll change, but that's for her to decide."

"I just miss her," I sob.

"I know you do." She stops rubbing my back. "But for now you should really find something to take your mind off of it. How about you come walk around the town with me?" she suggests.

"I don't wanna go out," I say. The last thing I could handle right now would be running into Ava somewhere in town. I think I'd probably lose it completely if I saw her.

"Ok, well, I'll bring you up some food in a little bit. Let me know if you need anything." She stands up from the bed, giving my shoulder one solid pat before leaving the room. I hear the door close behind her. As soon as it does, I'm sobbing uncontrollably again. With my body heat inside the blanket turning my bed into a warm cocoon, I drift off to sleep.

✦

When I wake up later, I poke my head outside of the blanket. I can't tell how long I was asleep but the light in the room and long shadows make me think it's probably somewhere in the afternoon. I still feel completely exhausted and my stomach growls. I can't remember the last time I ate anything. But just as I'm thinking that, I get a whiff of something from downstairs.

I pull the blanket off my bed and wrap it around me, covering the pajamas I'm wearing. I step out into the hallway and walk downstairs, the end of the blanket dragging along the floor behind me. In the living room, I find the source of the smell. Mom is cooking something in the large pan over the fire.

"You're cooking," I say.

She looks up and smiles at me. "I thought you might be hungry." She grabs a small plate from nearby and puts some of the food onto it before handing it over to me.

"What is it?"

"Bear," she says.

"Really?"

"Yup, we had some traders from up in the tundra pass through the city on their way south and I picked this up from them," she says.

I take a bite of the meat and it melts in my mouth. I suddenly realize just how hungry I am. I sit down on the sofa, plate in my lap, and continue to dig into the food. My mom smiles at me as I finish off the plate.

"It was really good," I say quietly.

"I'm glad you liked it. I'm putting the rest into the stew for later. I think it'll work well in there," she says, dropping pieces of the meat into the large black pot over the fireplace.

"It's the same stew?" I ask.

"Yeah, we can just keep adding stuff to it as we need. It's supposed to just keep making the flavors more intense over time. Just have to keep it above a certain temp," she explains.

"Huh, weird," I say. We sit in silence for another couple of minutes.

"You wanna do anything today?" she asks, breaking the silence first.

"Not really." I don't know what there even is to do in the city anymore. All the spots I can think of are completely gone. The library, the galleries, even the school buildings.

"Well, I heard they started construction over in the old city," she says.

"On what?"

"With so much of the lower levels gone, they're turning some of the old buildings into new stuff."

"Is there anything even left over there?"

"Of course! The buildings may be old and need a little repair but the actual structure of them is really solid. That old craftsmanship really does last forever," she says.

"Sounds interesting."

"You sure you don't wanna check it out with me?" She smiles. She really does know how to entice me.

"Fine," I say.

"Ok, good, go get changed and meet me back down here," she says.

I walk back up to my room and drop the blanket onto the bed, then I quickly change into the first outfit I see in my closet and walk back downstairs. My mom and I leave the house and start walking over to the old town.

She doesn't speak much. I think she can tell I'm still not really in the talking mood. And despite being out in the city again, I still can't stop thinking about Ava. Every time my mind goes back to her, I feel that pit in my stomach again.

We stop in front of one of the larger buildings on the street. Instead of a door it looks like it has a thick leather flap hanging in the doorway. There's noise coming from inside and a lot of people seem to be going in and out.

"What is this place?" I ask.

"Oh, this is the tavern. It's one of the oldest buildings in the city, and one of the only ones in the old city that was still being used regularly," she explains.

"Why're there so many people here?"

"Since the explosions, a lot of people have been without a home. They've been letting people stay there and helping to provide food and water to everyone. Them and the old scallop inn on the other side of the city," she says.

I look at the building again and then at the other ones on the street. There are a bunch of people carrying large wooden beams around and holding various tools. They seem to be working on repairing various parts of all the other buildings. There's one building I recognize; it's where I saw Saffron stealing a power cell from an android. People are carrying large amounts of machinery into the street from that building.

"What're they going to do with all that?"

"Probably get rid of it."

"Why would they get rid of all that old technology?"

"Well, without the grid there's not much point in keeping it around," my mom says.

"But what about what Dad's working on?" I ask.

She shakes her head. "Your dad has gone off the deep end."

"What do you mean?" I ask. He's been spending all his time either locked away in the lighthouse or out scouring the tundra, looking for a safe way down into the institute.

"I just mean that we have to prepare for the real possibility that this city won't get the grid back." She looks at the people working on the building. "And that's exactly what everyone here is doing."

I look out over the rest of the city again. People are working on buildings all around us but the rest of the city seems completely quiet and inactive.

I see the lighthouse far on the other side. It seems so distant now. I look to the other side and see the large cliffside I climbed with Ava for our school project to find that flower, and that's when I have a brilliant idea of how to get her to talk to me again. I'm going to bring her one of the edelweiss flowers.

I wake up early the next day and pack some things into a bag. I want to make sure I'm ready for the climb. I look out the window and there's a flurry of snow blowing. Seems to be much windier than a lot of the other days I've seen while here. I make sure to dress in as many layers as I can. I tug the bandages on my hand to make sure they're still wrapped tightly. My palm still hurts pretty bad and I haven't dared look at it yet.

I walk downstairs with my bag and I'm greeted by my mom in the living room.

"You heading out?" she asks.

"Yeah, I was gonna go watch the construction in the old town," I lie. She's been letting me go out more again, but I doubt she'd let me out if she knew where I was really going.

"You sure you wanna go out today? It seems colder than usual out there," she says.

"I just need to stretch my legs a little bit. Plus, I wanna watch more of the construction," I say.

"You want any company?" she asks, and I get nervous.

"I think I just wanna have a little time on my own today."

"Ok, well, I'll see you when you get home." She walks over and gives me a big hug. I hug her back before leaving the house. I walk along our street to the nearest set of stone steps and start heading down to the lower levels of June. I can feel the wind on my face as I get closer to the bottom of the city.

All of the wooden pillars with carvings along the side of the steps are covered with a thin layer of ice. It makes it much harder to make out what each carving is. Maybe they can get someone to clear the ice off of them soon.

When I reach the lowest level, I look around. It doesn't look like a single building made it through the destruction. I walk past where the docks used to be and see charred planks of wood sticking out of the ice. Next to them is the frame of one of the busses, halfway sunken into the ice, the tail end sticking high into the sky.

I continue past the old docks, towards the cliff face on the south side of June. I find the path that Ava showed me when we first came here and start walking up it, staying close to the rock so the wind doesn't push me around as much. Even with my thick coat I can still feel the chill blowing through it. It makes my hand feel even stiffer than before.

The climb up takes much longer on my own. Partly from the harsh weather but I also think it just feels like longer without Ava here to talk to. It's almost impossible to keep my mind from thinking of her. After a while of climbing, I reach the plateau with the small bench.

I look out over the city. It's my first time seeing the destruction from this angle and it looks even worse now that I can see it all. I don't think I had really wrapped my head around just how much of the city is gone. But from here it's crystal clear.

The wind at my back blows in from the ice shelf so I walk over to where the path continues and begin to climb up the steeper part of the rocks. I stumble on the rough ground as I try to squeeze between the two large boulders. The ice is slippery and the rocks under my feet are loose. A dangerous combo.

Going through this is much harder than the last time, but I keep trying to move forward. I slip again and catch myself on one of the rocks with my bandaged hand. As soon as my palm touches the rock, pain shoots up my arm, which causes me to stumble and fall face-first onto the icy rocks under my feet. I hold my arm for a couple of seconds until the pain subsides.

I pull myself up with my other hand and keep squeezing through the rocks until I finally reach the wall with the metal rungs embedded in it. I look up at the makeshift ladder and down at my bandaged hand. I grab one of the higher rungs with my good hand, pull myself up and step up onto the lower rung with my feet. It's slow progress inching up the wall this way and it takes all my effort not to get blown off by the wind.

Suddenly there's a massive gust and my body is pulled to the side. My instinct kicks in and I reach up with my bandaged hand to grab for another rung. The pain is overwhelming. It shoots up through my shoulder and fills my entire body. The shock loosens my grip and I slip away from the wall. I fall about ten feet, the wind completely knocked out of me.

What was that pain? That felt like more than just the cut on my palm. My entire arm is throbbing. I finally tug at the bandages and pull them off. The cold bites at my now exposed hand. I look down at where the cut was and, to my horror, see that the skin around the cut is almost fully transparent. I feel the spot with my other hand and it's as hard as stone. Was this from the crystal?

For now, I wrap the bandages back around my arm but no amount of hiding my hand can push down the grim thoughts I'm having about it. I need to get that flower first; I can deal with my hand afterwards. I pull myself up again, still trying to catch my breath. There are bruises over the rest of my body and a sharp pain in my head. I feel where the pain is coming from and when I pull my hand away there's a bit of blood. I wipe it away with my bandaged hand and walk back over to the makeshift ladder.

I'm much more careful climbing this time, making sure to only use my good arm. I finally reach the top and slide down over the lip of the crater and into the meadow of flowers. Just like last time, the crater seems to have completely blocked the wind. I lay in the plants for a couple of minutes, trying to recuperate from the fall.

The ground is warm against my back and the grass beneath me is soft. After the rough climb to get up here, I'm not in too much of a hurry to climb back down. I unwrap the bandages on my arm and look at the spot that's in pain. Without the snow blowing in my face, it's much easier to see, but that's a small comfort.

The skin around the cut is indeed transparent and when I hold it up above my face I can see the light filtering through. There are dark black veins running through the transparent part of the arm. I feel the skin with my other hand and it's completely hard all the way through. I try to move my fingers, but they respond slowly. Maybe there's a way to reverse this. It'll be fine, I'm sure.

I wrap the bandages back around my hand. When I get back down to June, I'll have to find Kai and see if she can help. I lower my arm and rest a little more. I try to feel the grass with my fingers and, while the feeling is still there, my fingers are considerably more numb than they used to be, almost like my arm has fallen asleep.

I finally stand up and look around for the reason I came here. The patch of grass I was lying on still has the imprint of where I had been. I push aside some of the larger bushes

and look around at the flowers growing near them. There are dozens of species that I've never seen before. I see bunches of orange berries growing on small bushes, deep orange flowers that look like butterfly wings, and even blue flowers that almost look like they're glowing. Maybe I can come back later and catalog some of these new plants another time.

Just as I'm thinking this, I spot the edelweiss flower across the crater near the edge of the willow tree. I kneel down next to it. There are a couple others growing nearby but this one looks the prettiest by far. I reach into my bag and pull out the glass jar I had brought with me.

The jar has a large crack running up the side of it, probably from when I fell earlier, but luckily it still seems to be mostly intact. I screw off the lid and scoop up some of the dirt the flower is growing out of, then gently drop it into the jar and screw the lid back on tightly. I hope this will keep it safe on the way back down.

I stand back up and place the glass jar carefully back into the bag. As I look up at the edge of the crater I slid down before, I instantly feel a sense of dread about climbing down. I pace around the crater, trying to get up the courage to do it.

As I'm walking in circles, trying carefully not to step on any of the other plants, my foot catches something beneath the grass. It's a small handle. I tap my foot on the ground around the handle and hear the echo of metal beneath me. Is there something below this?

I reach down and pull the handle. The grassy ground comes up with it and reveals a dark hole below. It looks like the plants grew right into the old metal hatch. I lay down and look into the hole. There's a thin spiral staircase going deep into the ground below and a series of tiny lights. Maybe this is another way out.

I lower myself down into the hatch and onto the stairs. These ones look almost identical to the ones we found in the institute but much narrower. I start walking down. As I get lower, the light from the hatch above begins to fade until the only light remaining is from the tiny red lights along the steps themselves. But at least I can still see where I'm walking.

The air down in this area smells stale and has a faint whiff of machinery too. I reach the bottom of the stairs and find myself in a small square room, no bigger than my room back at home. There's a dim light in the ceiling but nothing else in the room except a door. I pull it open.

On the other side is a massive room with a ceiling that stretches up far above me. The room goes far into the distance beyond. This must be what's inside the cliff at the edge of June. Up on the ceiling are massive hanging lights, brightly lighting up the entire length of the room.

All around me are old vehicles sitting in rows. They also stretch the length of the room but not a single one seems to be moving. Unlike most of the old vehicles I've seen, these ones are in almost perfect condition. I turn around to look down the other end. Instead of continuing on, there's a large metal door which stretches far up to the ceiling above me. I don't think I've ever seen anything quite as massive as this.

I walk up to this door and look for a way to open it. On one of the walls near the edge there's a box that says 'DOOR CONTROLS'.

"Could it really be that easy?" I say to myself. There's a small panel that swings open and a series of buttons inside. I notice one that says 'OPEN' which I quickly press. Suddenly the large metal door starts to swing open in front of me. I watch in awe as it moves and a bright light pours in through the crack in the door.

But just as suddenly as the door had started to swing open, there's a loud sound that echoes through the length of the room. All the lights flicker and then completely shut off; even the tiny lights that had lit my path along

the ground look like they've burned out too.
The door stops moving, still open a crack but
not moving any further than that. There's still
some light in the tunnels coming from above
but it doesn't seem to be from the same lights
as before. I guess opening it used up whatever
residual power was left in the system.

I walk over and squeeze through the
crack in the door. My eyes adjust to the light
and I find myself looking out over June.
There's a wooden sign next to me that says
WELCOME TO JUNE and a set of stone
steps leading down towards the city.

Just like all the others, these steps have
large wooden pillars next to them with carved
animals. Some look like bears, others like
birds, and all have the same reddish hue to the
wood that a lot of the old buildings in town
have. They're really pretty to look at up close.

As I get closer to the town, there are a
bunch of people walking around and suddenly
I recognize where I am. I'm in the Old Town.
People are continuing renovations on the
buildings and ahead of me I see the tavern my
mom and I walked by yesterday. I must've
done a full loop to get back here. When I have
more time, I'm going to have to go back and
draw up some new town maps with all the
stuff I've found.

I start walking back towards some of the
parts of town I'm more familiar with. I feel

some people looking at me as I walk by and realize I must look in pretty rough shape from that trip up. My whole body still feels completely sore all over, but I can barely think about that. All I want is to see Ava again.

I try to avoid anyone's gaze as I walk in the direction of Ava's house, but luckily most people seem to be focused on the rebuilding effort. I see a crowd carrying a large, black wooden beam. It looks like it had been part of one of the old buildings but I guess they're trying to reuse as much as they possibly can.

Maybe the Old Town is actually going to become popular again if they get it all fixed up. I walk down one of the sets of stone steps towards the lower levels of June on my way to see Ava. I'm suddenly nervous about giving her the flower. What if she won't even speak to me? Maybe I can just leave it on her doorstep.

I get to her street and there are a lot fewer people out walking. The sun is starting to set over the city too; I must've been gone almost the whole day. It sure flew by climbing up the cliffs. My stomach growls. Maybe I should just go get some food instead of seeing Ava.

I stop in my tracks.

No. I should go see her. I keep walking another few minutes until I arrive at her front door. I reach up with my good hand and knock. There are butterflies in my stomach as

I wait for someone to answer. The door swings open and Ava is standing there. She looks like she's been crying.

"Hey." I suddenly realize I have no idea what I actually want to say to her.

She tries to put on a stoic face. "What're you doing here?"

I think about what she said the last time we spoke, about how I hadn't listened to her. That I pushed her too far outside of her comfort zone. And I realize she was absolutely right. I look into her beautiful eyes.

"I just…I'm sorry," I stammer.

She looks at my face and her gaze softens. "What happened to you?" She reaches out and touches my forehead. I wince in pain as she touches the part that got scraped up when I fell.

"It's really no big deal." I try to play it off but I don't think she believes me.

"Still being reckless." Her words cut me like a dagger. I feel my eyes start to water so I try to look away. "What adventure was worth getting this beat up?"

"It…" I don't know if I should tell her now. I look back at her face and she looks like she's about to cry too. I reach into my bag and pull out the cracked glass jar with the edelweiss flower inside. "I wanted to give you this." I hand it to her.

She takes the jar from me and looks at the flower inside, then looks back at my face. "You climbed all the way back up there just for this?" she asks, tears in her eyes.

"I just...missed you," I say.

She gently places her hand on the back of my head and pulls me in, kissing me softly. Her lips feel soft and familiar. Tears run down my cheek as I kiss her back. Her hand pushes on the part of my head I hit earlier and it's a little painful, but my heart feels so full I barely notice it. We pull away from each other, still looking deeply into each other's teary eyes.

"I missed you too," she says.

"So, do you think you can give me another chance?" I ask hopefully, offering her the jar with the flower.

She pauses before responding, "I'm not sure. But maybe we could have dinner and talk about it."

I smile. "I'd love that."

"Ok, this weekend, then."

"Sounds like a plan." I lean in and give her one more small kiss on the cheek. She smiles at me as she closes the door. I float back towards my house again, hopeful about the possibility of starting over with her, and already planning out the perfect place for dinner.

REBUILDING

My mom and I sit in front of the fireplace in the early-morning hours, each reading a book while curled up in large blankets on our chairs. I'm reading an old book I found in the lighthouse called *The Odyssey*, which I picked because of the gold embossing on the cover but the story has me completely hooked.

The front door swings open and my dad enters in a flurry of snow. He's been spending all his days with Kai looking for a way down into the ruins of the institute.

"You find it?" I ask.

He comes over and sits down next to me. "Yes." He doesn't say anything more.

"How were things down there?" I can only imagine the state the facility was left in.

"It was pretty rough. That ship really did a number on all the stuff down there. Even the stairs down from the hatch were completely melted."

"How'd you get down, then?"

"We brought rope and climbing gear."

"Did you find the power cell?" I ask.

He sighs. "Yes and no."

"What do you mean?"

"It's fused inside the ship. And the crystal growth around it seems to have gotten even worse."

"What about Kai? Didn't she go up there with you?"

"She did, but she's heading back to the lighthouse to try and tackle our crystal problem."

"What're you going to do?"

"Well, if we can get that new power cell out from down there, I'm going to need to finish getting the electrical systems in the lighthouse updated." He doesn't sound optimistic.

"Do you need help?" I offer.

"Maybe later. We've decided to go ahead with our plan to construct a new lab up there and that's going to need a lot of my focus," he says.

More of his focus? It already feels like he's been gone so much.

"A new lab?" I remember the conversation I overheard between him and Kai a while back. I thought it was just something they were considering, but I didn't realize how serious they were about that idea.

"We're gonna build something up near the hatch on the tundra for Kai."

"For Kai?"

"Yeah, someplace she can study the crystals up close. And someplace where we can easily get down into that hatch to try and get the power cell out," he explains.

"And you're moving up there?"

"That's the plan. Kai even thinks we might be able to power the lab we're building up there using some of the crystals."

I remember the failed cells they had been trying back in the lighthouse. "I thought they weren't enough to provide power."

"Not the small ones we were using, but with ones as big as those down there, we might have better luck."

"What about us?" I look over at my mom, who gives a half-smile.

"Maybe I can build the new lab with some rooms for you two to stay in too, while I work." He smiles at us.

"That would be nice," Mom chimes in.

"Yeah, I wanna come up there too," I say.

"Well then, I better let the construction people know that we're gonna need some more help from them getting the place put together." I stand up to give him a hug and he softly pats me on the back. "Lots of work to be done." He walks back over to the door and is gone a second later.

"Your dad just keeps getting busier and busier."

"He's just trying to help," I say.

"Yeah, I know." She sounds a little defeated. I sit down next to her and she pulls me in close. We sit there without talking for a while until I feel a twinge in my arm.

"Mom?" I say softly.

"Yeah, sweetie?"

"I need to tell you something."

"Oh? What is it?"

I hesitate. I'd been dreading telling her about this. "You know those crystals Kai was researching?"

"Of course."

I hold my arm up and carefully pull the bandages off. My palm up through my wrist has turned entirely to the orange crystal, now so stiff I can't even bend my wrist anymore. The light from the fireplace shines through my hand, casting orange light on our faces. Mom reaches out towards my hand.

"Careful not to touch it," I warn and she recoils.

"How could you not tell me about this?" Her reaction is a mix of subdued anger and serious concern.

"I was hoping it would get better," I say timidly.

"How long has it been like this?"

"It's been painful since we got back from the institute," I say.

"But that was weeks ago."

"I know…but the crystallization only started two days ago."

"You really should have told me sooner." She looks over my arm with concern. "Have you talked to Kai about it yet?"

"Not yet."

"Ok, well your dad said she was over at the lighthouse, right? You should go talk to her," she says.

"Yeah, I will."

"Right now," she urges.

"Right now?"

Her eyes narrow at me. "Yes. You need to get that looked at right away."

"No, you're right." I stand up, wrapping the bandages back around my arm as I do.

"And as soon as you've talked with her you need to come right back and fill me in on what she says." We make eye contact, tears almost welling up in my eyes, and her gaze softens. "But how about this; later today when you come back, we can go shopping to find the perfect outfit for your date with Ava tonight?"

"Are there even shops around anymore?" Most of the market district was destroyed in the explosion.

"Of course! A bunch have relocated up the Old Town," she explains.

"Ok, I'll come meet you here after I see Kai," I assure her. I grab my coat off the peg by the door and pull it on over my shoulders. It's hard to move my hand through the sleeve but eventually I manage to get it on. And only with a little bit of pain.

"I'll see you when you get back," Mom says.

"Can't wait." I open the front door and step onto the street. The city feels so quiet compared to a few weeks ago. The crowds that used to walk around the streets have disappeared. Now it's only a scattered assortment of people.

Hopefully Kai is still over at the lighthouse when I get there. I look down below and see a couple of buses parked near the old docks, with crowds gathered around them. They must be getting ready to leave the city too. We really won't have many people left after too much longer.

The lighthouse casts a long shadow on the ground behind it as I approach. It seems to be the only part of this town that hasn't changed. The large metal door is locked when I get there so I pound my fist on it. It swings open and Kai looks surprised to see me.

"Olivia? What're you doing here?"

"Hey, sorry to barge in like this. Can I ask you about something?"

"Of course, what do you want to talk about?" She moves aside and I step into the lighthouse. We sit down at one of the nearby tables together.

"Can you tell me anything about the crystals you were studying?" I ask.

"The crystals? Why would you want to know about something like that?" She looks confused.

"I just really want to know more about them," I say. She narrows her eyes but continues anyways.

"Well, I still don't know too much about them. We found them growing up around the city a couple of decades ago,"

"That long ago?" I ask.

She nods. "Yeah, that's why I came up to June in the first place. I had been a professor of geology in University and heard rumors about strange crystal structures up this way, so I came to study them."

"What did you find?" I ask.

"Whatever the crystal is, it's new. No books have any information about anything like it. It also seems to have a tremendous amount of power in it," she explains.

"What kind of power?"

"Well, anytime it gets heated up, it releases massive amounts of energy. It's tough to observe without too much equipment so I'm not sure what's actually causing it. And I only really ever experimented with small pieces."

"Is it dangerous?"

She nods again. "You saw what happened to the town, right? Clearly that wasn't just from those ship's engines alone. But there's a bigger question that we should probably answer."

"What's that?"

"Why do you really want to know so much about the crystals?"

I'm nervous again as I hold up my arm with the bandages around it. She stares at it and from the look on her face I'm pretty sure she's figured me out.

"Please tell me that's not what I think it is." She pulls out a thick pair of rubber gloves and puts them on.

"What do you think it is?"

"You touched one of them, didn't you?" She looks deeply concerned as I unwrap the bandages, revealing the crystal structure growing through my arm.

"Do you think you can fix it?" I hold out my arm to Kai and she grabs it. Her rubber gloves make weird noises as they rub against my arm. Her grip is tight, however I can't seem to feel it at all.

"How'd this happen?" She turns my arm around and looks through the crystal structure.

"I cut it on a shard," I explain.

She lets go of my arm. "That must be why it's spreading so quickly."

"Is there anything you can do for it?" I lower my arm onto the table between us. It hits with a loud thunk. My fingers still move, but just barely.

"I don't know. I've studied these crystals for decades and I still barely understand anything about them." She must notice the worried look on my face. "But I'll try everything I can possibly think of to help reverse this."

"That means a lot," I say.

"Does it hurt?" She pulls off her rubber gloves and sets them down on the table.

"Yes."

"I'm sorry, I can get you something to help with the pain." She gets up from the table and walks over to a large cabinet. She opens the doors and pulls out a small metal case.

"What's that?" I ask.

"It's medicine, made from some of the flowers that used to grow up here," she explains as she walks back over to the table. She sets the jar down in front of us. "Drink a little bit of this every morning. It'll help a little but you'll likely still feel some pain in that arm."

I grab the jar. "And it'll help reverse it?"

She pauses. "Well, no. I don't know how to reverse it yet."

"So what should I do?"

"Most importantly, don't let anyone touch your arm. Anyone that does is going to have the same thing start to happen to them. And in the meantime, I'm going to work on figuring out how to stop the growth of crystals."

"What about my dad?" I ask.

"His project can wait." She smiles at me and my worry about the crystals on my arm starts to melt away.

"What should I do now?" I ask.

"Go lie down for a little bit. I'll come get you if I make any progress."

"What're you going to do?" I ask.

"Honestly, we're in a bit of a desperate place so I figure it's Hail Mary time." She walks over to another desk and sits down in front of it. There are containers with the crystals inside scattered across it. She pulls on her gloves again and starts taking crystals out of their boxes, carefully placing them on the table.

I watch as she walks back and forth to the large cabinet on the other side of the room, pulling out a series of weird-looking tools. She grabs one of the large tools and scrapes it against a crystal. It makes a loud screeching noise which fills the room and makes me shiver. She stops and puts the tool down, examining the crystal closely afterwards.

I sit in one of the big chairs on the other side of the room and let my eyes close. I listen as Kai continues trying things with the crystals until I drift off to sleep.

✦

I'm woken by a hand on my shoulder and a soft voice.

"Hey, dear. I think I found something," Kai says. I slowly open my eyes and see her standing above my chair.

"Wait, really?" I ask.

"Well, it's better than nothing," she says. I get up and she leads me over to the table she's been working at.

"What do you have?" I look at the assortment of equipment.

She picks up a syringe of green liquid with a long, intimidating needle on the end. My heart beats a little faster as I stare it down.

"Will it hurt?" I ask.

"Yes, I'm sorry," she says.

I roll up my sleeve with some help from her. There's a sharp pain as she jabs me with the needle. I grit my teeth. Finally, she's done, and she wraps a small bandage around my upper arm. I roll my sleeve down again.

"So this will reverse it?" I ask.

She's silent again as she puts the needle back. "That'll slow the spread a bit. But it won't stop it completely."

I look down at my bandaged palm. "So what do I do?"

"Look, kid, I'm gonna do everything I can to reverse this, ok?"

I fake a smile but her words don't do much to alleviate the feeling of dread that's come over me. She puts a hand on my shoulder.

"I want you to come check in with me tomorrow," she says.

"I will," I assure her.

Neither of us says anything more but she pulls me in for a big hug before sitting back down at her workbench with the other containers of orange crystals. I gather up my things and leave the lighthouse, trying to ignore the numbing feeling spreading through my arm as I make my way home.

I reach my house and quickly go inside, only to find Mom in nearly the same spot she was this morning, engrossed in the book she's reading. Also much further along in it than she was earlier.

"You were gone a while." She looks up at me, faking a smile, but I can see the concern behind it.

"I spoke to Kai."

"And?" She shuts her book and stands up, looking over my arm.

"She gave me something to help," I say.

Mom looks somewhat doubtful as she glimpses the orange crystal still on my wrist. "It's going to stop?"

"She's still working on that part," I say sheepishly.

"Well, she's one of the smartest people I know. I want you checking in with her regularly, ok?"

"Yeah, I'm going back tomorrow morning," I say, still overcome with dread.

"How about we take a shopping trip? Help take your mind off things?" she asks.

"Weren't we always going to do that?" I joke.

"Yes, but now we have even more reason to." She grabs her coat from near the door and pulls it on. "Let's head out to the shops."

We walk over to the Old Town together. A lot of progress has been made on the buildings here in the past couple of days. All the broken windows have been replaced with thick wooden shutters, each carved with detailed patterns.

"It's really changed here," I note as we walk past the buildings. There are still a number of people working around us.

"Yeah, well, there's not much else left to do around June so most people have been chipping in when they can," my mom says. We stop in front of a large building that's being repaired. A couple of people are working on the roof, helping to repair some of the large holes.

"What's this place?" The building stretches down the street, and every couple of feet is another set of doors.

"It's the old market," Mom says. "When the city got bigger, they expanded to that new market district."

"How do you know about that?" I ask.

"I've been doing research about the city. There's a lot of info out there about the old town."

We walk in through one of the open doorways. Inside the building is a long hallway that seems to stretch the entire length of the building. It's a complete mess inside. Boxes are stacked all along the walls, various tools have been left around everywhere, and large wooden beams lay across the hallway. Light comes in from the holes in the ceiling.

I look around at all the chaos. "What're they making this place into?"

"It's going to be the new market," she explains, ushering me along the hallway. We step over some of the large beams. Another is being pulled up towards the ceiling with a series of ropes and pulleys. We duck under it and keep walking.

As we get further in, there's less construction and considerably less light. This part doesn't have holes in the ceiling anymore, and though there are lanterns hanging from the beams above, even with their light the room is still pretty dim. There's a series of small stalls that have been set up on either side of the hallway, each one stacked with various goods. I recognize some of the people behind the stalls from the shops in the market.

"Everyone's still setting up, but Tove told me she'd be ready for customers today," Mom says. She waves at people as she passes by them.

"Who's Tove?"

"She used to have the little clothing shop down in the market. Oh, here she is."

We stop at one of the stands. There're piles of neatly folded clothing stacked on a small counter, with more hanging on the wall. There's a woman behind the counter, rummaging through a series of wooden boxes, which also seem to be full of clothing. She notices us when we walk up.

"What can I help—" She stops when she sees my mom, "Oh, hey there, Victoria." She looks at me, "And you must be Olivia. I've heard so much about you,"

"Hey," I say.

"Nice to see you again, Tove. The move go ok?" Mom asks.

"Yeah, still getting used to this new space. Feels a little weird," Tove says.

I look through the clothing as the two of them catch up. The patterns here look like stuff from back home. Maybe it came in with the last trade shipment. I pull out a pair of bright plaid pants. They look kind of like the ones my mom gave me.

I keep looking. There are some warm sweaters in there that don't really seem to be my style. I pass by those and look up at the clothes hanging on the walls. They all look much fancier than the ones down on the table. As I'm looking, one of the dresses catches my eye. It's a long dress made from black fabric. I reach out and feel it; it's softer than anything I've ever owned. But the thing that really draws me to it is the pattern. Over the whole dress is a small print of flowers, specifically the edelweiss flower. It's perfect.

"Can we get this one?" I walk over and interrupt my mom and Tove with the end of the dress in my hand.

"Oh, that's a beauty, isn't it?" Tove grabs it from off the wall and holds it up in front of her. "It came all the way from down south. Apparently, it's all the rage for fancy parties these days," she says.

"You mind if we take that one Tove?" Mom says.

Tove smiles at her and then looks at me. "It's all yours," she says, handing the dress back to me. It feels heavy in my arms as I fold it up. "You looking for anything else?" she asks.

I look up at my mom.

"Nah, I think we're all good with this," she says.

"Well, come back and visit soon," Tove says.

"I will." Mom gives her a hug before we head back the way we came. Tove gives us a wave, then returns to organizing her boxes. I really didn't think much about what my mom got up to when I wasn't home but it seems like she's been meeting a lot of people up here. We leave the building and make our way back to our house.

"How long have you known Tove?" I ask as we get back.

"What do you mean?" Mom asks. She takes off her coat and hangs it back up.

"I didn't know you were that close with anyone here," I say.

"She was one of the first people I met when I got up here."

"You never mentioned her." I take off my coat and hang it up next to hers.

"I don't mention everyone I meet," she says. "You know, I don't just sit around this house the whole day," she jokes.

"I know. I just didn't know you were so close with other people."

"I mean, your dad hasn't exactly been around since we've gotten up here. He's always so busy with his work. Even now, there's always something keeping him away." She seems sad, but then she smiles. "I'm glad you and Ava are talking again." She changes the subject abruptly and gives me a big grin, although I can still sense her sadness behind it.

"Yeah, me too. I'm gonna go get changed." I carry the dress through the living room and towards the stairs.

"Come down after and I'll do your hair," Mom calls after me.

I climb the stairs up to my room. It has become a bit of a mess, clothes on the floor, papers stacked up on the desk, and my bag from my trip up to get the flower for Ava still sitting there fully packed. I just haven't had the energy to unpack it yet.

I lay the new dress out on my unmade bed. As I change out of the clothes I was wearing, I notice how bruised my body still is. There's a large black and blue bruise covering most of my ribcage from where I fell on my side. I grab the dress and pull it on, carefully zipping up the side of it.

I look at myself in the mirror. The dress falls near my ankles and fits me almost perfectly. It looks just like I hoped it would. I spin around and the fabric of the skirt spins with me. The only part that clashes are the bandages wrapped around every inch of my arm.

I rummage around the bottom of my closet and pull out a pair of thick black boots. These should match perfectly. I pull the boots on, making myself at least an inch or two taller. Then I pull out an old black jacket and pull that on over the dress, hiding most of the bandages.

I walk downstairs in my new outfit. I hope Ava will like it. My mom is sitting in the living room and she smiles when she sees me.

"Oh, you look so beautiful, sweetie." She waves me over and I sit down on the stool in front of her. "So where are you two going?" she asks as she starts to braid my hair.

"We're gonna meet down by the ice shelf," I say.

"Why there?"

"I'm planning something special," I explain.

"Well, I hope you'll tell me about it afterwards." She pulls the hair from behind my ears and continues working.

"I promise I will."

My neck feels cool without all my hair on it. Mom pulls out ribbons and starts weaving them into the braids. She's only done this a couple of times before, since it takes a while. I sit quietly on the stool, and she hums softly as she works. I feel a final tug on my hair as she ties the ribbons together.

"There. You're all done," she says.

I walk over to the doorway and look at myself in the small mirror next to it. My hair looks so cool. It's been completely pulled back, with black ribbons woven into the braids along the side of my head.

"It looks awesome." I turn my head back and forth.

"I'm glad you like it. And I can't wait to hear all about your date later," she says. I run over and give her a big hug. As I pull away, I catch her looking at the bandages around my hand with concern. She doesn't say anything, but I can tell exactly what she's thinking. Probably because I've been thinking the same thing myself.

"I'll see you later." I try to brush off the feeling of dread with a smile as I grab a large bag from near the door and throw it over my shoulder. Mom gives me a smile as I make my way out the door and down the stone steps towards the bottom level of the city.

Most of the chaos that has been happening in the town has completely died down now. I think Dad said close to eighty percent of everyone moved out. And the buses only come once a week instead of every day.

I reach the empty part of the town and continue down the steps. I wonder if they're gonna do anything with this whole area. Maybe they can rebuild some of the buildings and bring some more people back to the town. In just a few weeks, June has gone from a major metropolis to somewhere no bigger than a small village.

The lowest street seems completely unchanged since the last time I was down here. I look down at the ice shelf and see the square patch of ice that I cleared off yesterday. The ice is almost completely level with the street now. I take the bag off my shoulder and carefully place it on the ground. I unzip it and check to make sure the ice skates inside are ok. I managed to scavenge them from the wreckage, so they're a little beat up, but they should still work.

I look out over the ice again, at where the docks used to be. It still feels like just yesterday that I was arriving to June on one of the buses. I still can't believe everything that's happened since then. I look out further beyond the ice shelf and wonder what other stuff is out there.

"Hey there," a voice says from behind me. I turn and see Ava. She's wearing a deep navy dress and her hair is down. Behind her ear is tucked the edelweiss flower I had given her. There's a big smile across her face and I feel my cheeks turning red.

"You look beautiful," I tell her.

"You do too." She leans in and gives me a soft kiss. "So what adventure are we going on today?" She smiles as I hold up the pair of ice skates for her.

"I thought we could go ice skating again before dinner."

She takes the skates from me. "I think that sounds absolutely perfect."

We hold hands and walk out onto the ice together. I feel the warmth of her hand in mine, and everything feels right again. I squeeze her hand tightly as I imagine our next adventure together.

Acknowledgements

After being in the works for nearly four years, it's surreal to finally see Edelweiss out in the world. My life has changed in so many ways since I wrote the first draft of this book and there are so many people who helped get this book to where it is today.

As always, I have to thank my family for their constant support through everything in my life. I love you all so much and you mean the world to me.

I'd like to thank my incredible editor Jess Lawrence for helping to polish this story. Your feedback and guidance has helped make not just this book, but all my books what they are.

I'd also like to thank my two incredible artists Minna Ollikainen and Abigail Spence for helping to bring this book to life with your art. I'm always honored to work with you both and see the breathtaking art you make.

A special thanks to my writing club for helping to keep me inspired and setting the bar so high for me. Being surrounded by so many amazing writers helps drive me to become a better writer myself.

And lastly, thank you to everyone who's read my books. Whether this is the first one you've picked up, or you've read the full series, it means the world that you're supporting an indie author like myself. I truly hope that you've enjoyed reading this book as much as I've enjoyed writing it. Now it's on to the final book in the series!

ABOUT THE AUTHOR

Lloyd Hall grew up in the small coastal town of Short Beach, Connecticut and now lives a cozy life in California. His childhood was filled with fantastical stories and he often found himself lost in books from the local library. He channeled his childhood love of stories into the Wardenclyffe Series and is proud to present the third book, Edelweiss.

www.lloyd-parker-hall.com